Linda Watson

Fifty Weeks
of Green

Linda Watson is a food evangelist and wife based in west Raleigh, North Carolina. Since early childhood, she has obsessed about many things, including romance books, gardening, and politics. She has put nothing on hold except housework, which is why this book is in your hands now.

She is also the author of *Wildly Affordable Organic: Eat Fabulous Food, Get Healthy, and Save the Planet—All on $5 a Day or Less.*

Fifty Weeks of Green

FIFTY WEEKS
of GREEN

Romance & Recipes

Linda Watson

Dear Jean —
Thanks so much for
testing recipes for 50 Weeks!
You encouraged me to leave
the skin on the sweet-potato
fries & make other
essential changes.
Hugs to you &
your dogs!

Cook for Good | Raleigh, North Carolina

Linda Watson

see p. 174 too!

for Bruce,
my partner in love on this amazing journey

THE FIRST BOX

I grimace at myself in the mirror as I cram a dusty hiking hat over my cascade of curly black hair. Damn Saturdays, damn my Italian ancestors, and damn Charlotte Conover for sticking me with her CSA box today. Just because the keynote speaker for some foodie festival canceled at the last minute and she had to fly to San Francisco was no reason to stick me with a box of arugula and beets.

"Please Sophia?" she'd crooned. "Don't let all those organic vegetables rot on a shelf somewhere. They need to get out — and so do you!"

I fight through Christmas traffic to the mall. They've put up a huge Christmas tree over the underground parking entrance. How odd to drive beneath such a huge tree, park next to a Target, and then ride an escalator to the farmers' market! I grab the reusable box from last week's order and curse again as the wind sweeps receipts for my farewell expense report under nearby cars. I grab up the papers I can find, resettle my hat, and ride up to the square.

Blinking in the bright sunlight, I scan the red and green banners with all the hopeful, helpful names. Bah, humbug! The economy is in the toilet, the planet is heating up, and I haven't gotten laid in forever. Not since IBM summoned Kenny back to East Fishkill to help with that superchip. Why couldn't Charlotte just skip the kumbaya and thaw frozen blocks of food like everyone else? But she was my roommate at NC State and had been my best friend for nearly thirty years. She'd rescued me from so many jams that the least I could do was rescue her pet produce.

I finally spot a table heaped with boxes marked Bee's Knees Farm. I push my way through the tangle of adults yakking on cell phones, their holiday-frenzied children and bulky cloth bags of potatoes clogging the sidewalk in front of the farm stands. Some farmers are already taking down their displays, so I try to pick up my pace without seeming like a Grinch.

Even Farmer Bee or whatever he calls himself has his back to the crowd, reaching up to take down the chalkboard hawking this week's offerings. His flannel shirt strains against a back rippling with muscles, coming out of his work-worn jeans just enough to give a glimpse of bare hip and waist. He is lean and sleek, like an otter or one of the boys I used to frolic with back when Charlotte and I were wild young things bent on exploring the wonders of our co-ed dorm. Hadn't I heard on NPR just last week that most farmers were over fifty and getting older every season?

"Thank you *so much* for donating to Help for the Hungry!" a perky voice practically squeals right behind me. As I turn to look at the squeaky blonde, I step between a corgi and his master, getting tangled up in the leash. Bam! I'm down on my hands and knees. The corgi's person apologizes as the blonde volunteer bends to help me up.

I bite back yet another curse, knees and spirits stinging. What a week. First the senator dumps me and now I dump myself. Palms still on the pavement, I see well-worn work boots in front of me. I rise slowly, cheeks blazing with embarrassment and a hot flash working its way across my chest and down my spine. I look straight ahead to avoid the stares of the curious crowd, but also to enjoy the way well-used denim drapes strong thighs and lean hips.

"Didn't Wendell Berry write something about *our bodies live by farming; we come from the earth and go back to it?*" drawls Farmer Bee. His voice reminds me of James Taylor. Maybe he grew up in Chapel Hill, like the singer did. "You OK down there, Sugar?"

I gasp as I meet his eyes. He's no kid, just built like one. His short black hair is streaked silver at the temples. Smile lines show he's fifty-something, but had a good time getting there. His deep green eyes hold mine a little longer than is comfortable, but maybe he's just worried that I'll sue him.

"It's Sophia, not Sugar. I'm, I'm here for Charlotte Conover's box," I manage to say. "Am I too late?"

"No, *Sophia*, you're fine. Just fine," he says, looking me up and down. "Sure you're not hurt? Maybe you shouldn't wear Lady Gaga platforms when you come out here to the wilderness."

"It was the dog, not the shoes. And these are more Katy Perry than Gaga. Practically sensible, given that we're in a mall."

"OK, ruin my pastoral illusions. I'm Roger Branch, in charge of the agriculture that your friend Charlotte is supporting." He slides the last box on the table toward me. "Here's her share for the week, with lots of greens and roots. I've even tucked in the last jar of honey for the year."

"I hope I can figure out what to do with all these leafy things while she's out of town," I say. The open box fills me with vague dread. "What's this?" I pick up what looks like a very long, thick white carrot with a wild spray of rough leaves at the end.

He laughs. "That's a daikon, a Japanese radish. Mostly you just chop it, cook the leaves, and eat the white part raw. There are plenty of recipes online. Just remember the prime directive here at Bee's Knees Farm: don't waste a scrap."

"But there's so much here!"

"Start with a salad and a honey-mustard dressing tonight. In a few minutes you'll have a salad so tender you could feed it to angels."

"Promise?"

"Promise. I bet you'll want to come back next Saturday to sign up for your own box." He looked at me intently, seeming to offer more than a weekly supply of veg. "One of my supporters just got transferred, so we've got an open subscription."

"No thanks, I don't cook. I'm too busy and really, I'd rather just nuke something and get on with my life."

"Cooking *is* life, Sugar. Like eating and love."

"Please call me Sophia, Farmer Branch. I'll think about it. But if this is all arugula, you'd better have a refund ready!"

"We don't usually do refunds with CSAs, but for you I'll keep some money on hand. For your part of the deal, dress so you can stay upright. Leave those silly shoes at home so you don't break an ankle picking up your beets."

I snort and grab the box, surprised at how heavy it is. I'll wear my favorite boots with the slightly sturdier heels if I ever come back. Why didn't Charlotte warn me?

Still, I can't resist picking up a Homewood poinsettia for Mamma from Logan Trading Company's amazing display. I'll bring it to her when we have our Christmas Eve feast.

I ride the escalator back down to parking level two and strap the poinsettia in the passenger seat. The box of veg goes in the trunk, next to the box with my Talking Heads mug and collection of horse statues that the senator's chief of staff watched me pack up after she gave me the ax. I couldn't bear to bring it inside yesterday.

"We wouldn't have squeaked through to win this time without you," she'd told me. "Nobody knows how to sift data better to find undecided voters who might pull the lever for the Good Guys. But re-districting makes this race a done deal."

It was the same story everywhere in North Carolina, for both parties. No risk, no donations, no jobs.

I schlep in the work box and then vegetables. Yes, there's a lot of arugula and that scary daikon, but also beets, carrots, collards, tender spring onions, and some leafy bunches I don't recognize. At least there's plenty of room in the fridge. Diet soda, OJ, take-out containers, and a collection of hot sauces on the top; celery and oranges in the drawers.

I put most of my haul in the fridge, then take my time making a salad. This lettuce is not a hard, tight ball like the iceberg lettuce Mamma used to cut into wedges and top with blue-cheese dressing. The leaves are loose, more like big rose petals. Each is washed in color, from pale green near the stem to reddish brown on the edges. I rinse a leaf and take a bite. It's tender and succulent, nothing like the travel-weary mesclun that gives salad bars a bad name.

I google *honey mustard dressing*. Thousands of recipes appear, some saying you need to use a non-reactive container. I google again. Turns out a glass jar will work fine and ceramic would too. The trick is to avoid aluminum, copper, or cast iron. If you don't, the vinegar will leach out the metal and make the dressing taste like a suit of armor.

I lick the honey spoon and scroll through the recipes. Maybe I *do* need to start cooking, now that I have all this free time and no money. Maybe Farmer Bee wants to barter.

Honey-Mustard Dressing

Mix up a quarter-cup of prepared mustard and two tablespoons each of honey, apple-cider vinegar, and water in a non-reactive container. Keep any extra in the fridge.

CHRISTMAS NIGHT

I hang up my keys and tap the jingle bell dangling next to them for a little cheer. Christmas at Mamma's in Asheville had been quiet without her sister Donatella to cook and make us laugh. Now my apartment seems even quieter. I should have bought a poinsettia for myself at the market too.

I microwave the leftover Stouffer's lasagna that Mamma sent home with me. It is no match for the multi-layered wonder that Zia Donatella made every Christmas Eve. Mamma always chipped in money from extra holiday-season jobs after Papà left, but she'd never learned to cook.

I put my plate in the dishwasher, turn on the radio, and try on the new jacket Mamma gave me. It was a little too tight, like every garment she'd given me since I was twelve. I still had the big eyes and full lips of my namesake Sophia Loren, but time had thickened my hourglass figure. Maybe I should listen to Mamma and start warming up Lean Cuisines instead of Hungry-Man frozen dinners.

I hang up the jacket and pull on my red-and-white Wolfpack sweatshirt instead. Might as well clean now so the place will be ready when Charlotte comes over for our annual Christmas viewing of *It's a Wonderful Life*.

I start with my work box, putting the horse statues on the window ledge so they can see out over the greenway. My Talking Heads coffee mug makes me ask David Byrne's big question again, "How did I get here?"

Underneath the mug, I see part of the answer. A thick engraved invitation to the Senator's fall fundraiser shows the names of the biggest sponsors, grouped in the usual gold, silver, and bronze categories.

Shakey red circles around five of the thirty names showed who had pledged but not paid. I'd added three exclamation points next to *Mr. and Mrs. Bob Thwaite*. Despite warnings to the Senator, this was the second event in a row where they got public thanks for being donors without writing even the smallest check. Bob made multiple trips to the buffet table and open bar, but never covered his part of the caterer's bill. He networked with the Senator's real supporters, the ones who made events like this worthwhile and who might invest in one of Thwaite's projects. But this year, parasites like Thwaite meant the Senator couldn't pay me to research complex issues between campaigns.

I take the elevator downstairs to the Harris Teeter to get the makings for the dip that kept Charlotte and me fueled through term papers and finals. Lately, I've been eating it for dinner with a diet soda. It wasn't exactly antipasto, but it sure was fast and filling.

Hot Bean Dip
Active time: 5 minutes. Total time: 8 minutes. Serves 2.

one 16-ounce can refried black beans
½ cup Frontera Chipolte salsa
zest of one lime

Put beans and salsa in a microwave safe bowl, cover, and microwave on high until nearly hot, about 3 minutes. Stir and heat for another minute or so until hot. Taste and add more salsa if needed. Zest lime on top of hot bean dip.

Serve hot with corn chips or vegetable sticks.

LET'S MAKE A DEAL

Flicka whinnies four times, falls silent, then whinnies again. I fumble through the reading glasses and paperbacks on my bedside table and stroke my phone to quiet her. Good girl — it's time to go exchange Charlotte's empty CSA box for a full one and talk with Farmer Bee about our possibilities together.

Work possibilities, that is. And I sure need work possibilities. Why do so many layoffs happen between Thanksgiving and Christmas? The practice gives new meaning to Black Friday. It's hard on the holiday spirit and hard to get another job while the gainfully employed swill their eggnog and hang mistletoe over the printer.

I shower and dry my hair, bending over to get a little Loren-like height in the crown. I slide into my winter uniform of black turtleneck, black jeans, and black high-heeled boots. Because this is practically a job interview, I take an extra minute to put on eye liner and rose berry lipstick. And because there may be dirt involved, I top it all off with my gray tweed coat, the one I wore when walking Kenny's dog. I realize with a start that I miss Ranger more than I miss his master.

I put the folder with my sketches in Charlotte's CSA box and head for the elevator, car keys jingling. What a pain in the butt to have to drive to the mall that I can see from my balcony! But I can't imagine fighting across busy Six Forks Road lugging boxes of veg.

As I drive down into the mall's parking deck, my headlights strike the big black-and-white Calvin Klein posters that are this season's ad displays. Gorgeous, barely clad girls are further undressing thoroughly-waxed studs, opening a shirt here and slipping a thumb inside a waistband there. *Jeez, get a room!* When did advertising become porn? And how long has it been since I wanted to tear somebody's clothes off?

The brisk wind cools my cheeks as I ride the escalator up to the Midtown Farmers' Market. The scene is as vivid as a child's drawing, with white tents on three sides of a dazzling green square.

Big planters full of multi-colored pansies mark the corners. A broad sidewalk surrounds the square on three sides, with a Starbucks on the fourth. Parents field stray balls between sips of coffee as their toddlers play.

Twenty or so booths offer food and crafts across the sidewalk. Beyond them, shops sell fashionable goods more modern than their facades imply. The cineplex and hotel are set back from the core of this modern village, but it's still clear we're not in Jolly Olde England. Just as well. I'm grateful for democracy, modern dentistry, and delivery pizza.

I pick out Roger from among the other twenty or so booths offering food and crafts. Under his white tent, Roger describes this week's share from Bee's Knees Farm to a plump blonde woman in more makeup than should be legal in broad daylight. When he shows her the salad mix with spicy sorrel and licorice-tinged chervil, she claps with delight. Her elaborate Christmas sweater jingles. I don't clap, but I do admire the red, yellow, and hot-pink stems of some tropical-looking leaves next to the salad mix.

"Rainbow chard," says Blondie with another jingle. "Roger, you are a darlin'! See you next week." She balances her box with several shopping bags as she walks away.

For a moment, Roger and I look at each other while the tent flaps in the brisk winter breeze.

"Did you get my proposal?" I finally ask him, wanting to get this over with one way or the other. I'm much more comfortable with numbers and graphics than negotiations. I emailed the file Wednesday night and hadn't heard back. Maybe Roger didn't actually check his email. Maybe his spam filter had taken it for one of those phony pleas for banking help.

"I got it. But not sure that I get it. Seems like what I've been doing has been working just fine."

"Then why do you still have a slot in your winter CSA left? Coon Rock Farm and Edible Earthscapes sold out by Halloween. And it's not just one slot, either, is it? Charlotte told me you've got ten left."

"Twelve," he said sheepishly, looking down at his boots. The wind pressed his denim jacket close to his broad shoulders. "But I'm making it. It's better than last year."

"Products don't sell themselves, not even this gorgeous lettuce. You've got to let people know what you've got and why they should want it." I spread out my sketches, showing more ideas for telling the farm's story.

Our hands brush as we scramble to keep the pages from blowing away. "I'll do a little website and a Facebook page with links to recipes that work. There are too many confusing duds online. 'Use a non-reactive container'? Why not just say 'use glass or ceramic'? Or warn people about vinegar? We could even ask your current supporters to share their favorite recipes and tips."

"And you'll do all this in exchange for a box of produce every week?"

"Yes, if you'll let me finish out the season. It will take time to set up, but then should be pretty easy to keep going. I can even show you how to do it yourself, if you want."

Roger chuffs, but looks at the pages thoughtfully. His green eyes meet mine and hold them, looking long and hard as if evaluating my very character. Finally he shrugs and lets one corner of his mouth rise into a crooked grin.

"Maybe. I'll think about it. But first there's something you need to think about too." He takes a wooden box the size of a briefcase out from under the table. It's a small miracle of cabinetry, with dovetailed corners and the silhouette of a tree —
maybe an oak? — inlaid on the lid. It looks old but beautifully cared for. He lifts the lid and pulls out a straw-colored envelope made of heavy, textured paper.

"Joining a CSA is not like buying a pair of silly shoes that you can wear once and then leave in your closet with all the other things you bought but don't use. It's a commitment. And I don't spend my life force or share the life force of my farm with folks who don't support, I mean really support, what we do."

"I get it. Charlotte said she paid upfront for six months of veg."

"It's not just the money," he said with a hint of a growl. "We're doing something important here. That's why you need to read, understand, and commit to this contract first."

"Contract? Look, I'll just do the design work for a month, you keep me in veg, and we'll see how it goes after that."

"No! No, that's not how I work. Read this and come back next week. You can ask any questions you like, but only start up with me if you are serious about the food and the work."

He clears his throat and shifts to put his back to the December wind. "If you decide to sign, we'll change the commitment period from twenty-five weeks to twelve. That should give you enough time to fill up my spring subscription list. If we decide to go on from there, we'll add an addendum."

I take the contract and Charlotte's box. Did she sign this thing too? *Toto*, I think, *we're not in Kroger anymore!* I don't even like vegetables, but suddenly I want to be seen as worthy of this man's offerings as much as I once wanted a pony for Christmas. On the square, the Salvation Army volunteer rings his bell in time with my heartbeat.

Back at home, I center the envelope on the kitchen island and make another salad from the bag of salad mix in Charlotte's box, glad she encouraged me to help myself. While I nibble the tender, spicy greens, I research dressing recipes and come up with my own variation, using sorghum from a gingham-topped jar that I picked up from another booth.

Zia Donatella always said to cook from sweet to savory and from dry to wet so you could reuse measuring spoons and cutting boards. I bet she'd measure the vinegar before anything sticky! For that matter, why not just use her old kitchen scale so I don't have to use a measuring spoon at all?

Sorghum-Mustard Dressing
Active time: 3 minutes. Total time: 3 minutes. Serves 5.

¼ cup prepared bold or yellow mustard (60 grams)
2 tablespoon apple cider vinegar (30 grams)
2 tablespoons water (30 grams)
2 tablespoons sorghum (42 grams)

Mix all ingredients in a small glass jar or other non-reactive container. (Vinegar reacts with aluminum, cast iron, and copper, giving the dressing an unpleasant metallic taste.) Shake or stir to mix.

Refrigerate any extra. This dressing thickens as it chills and keeps for weeks.

THE CONTRACT

Fortified with an espresso and a warm, gooey square of Charlotte's chocolate flip cake, I settle into the chintz-covered swivel rocker, angling it so I could look out over Midtown to the pines and bare oaks along the greenway. I squint at my lucky horse statues prancing along the window ledge, imagining them happy in a tree-ringed pasture.

The flap of the envelope was tucked inside, not sealed. I pull out two identical documents, printed on crisply folded, subtly textured paper. Important paper, the type a top architect might use for a resume. A cartoon bee flies over the top of each page.

Bee's Knees Farm
Silk Hope, North Carolina
MUTUAL SUPPORT AGREEMENT

Roger Wyatt Branch and Bee's Knees Farm (hereinafter known as "the Farmer") agrees to provide a weekly box of produce to Sophia Verde (hereinafter referred to as "the Supporter") as outlined below.

RULES FOR THE SUPPORTER

Understanding:

The Supporter agrees to join the Farmer in the dance with Nature that is the essence of agriculture, with all the risks and rewards entailed. The Supporter understands the contents of the box shall reflect the seasons and weather as well as the skill, diligence, and luck of the Farmer.

Payment:

The Supporter shall pay $500 for a full share or $300 for a half share. This fee is not

refundable, even if the farm experiences crop
failure or other disasters.

Pick Up:

The Supporter shall pick up the box every
Saturday during normal market hours. Any box not
picked up shall be donated to Help the Hungry or
a similar organization or needy family selected
by the Farmer.

Storage:

The supporter shall store the produce prop-
erly to avoid waste.

Preparation:

The supporter will use all possible parts of
the produce, including stems and peels normally
discarded by spendthrifts. Food shall be consumed in an orderly manner to avoid loss due to
spoilage.

Commingling:

The supporter is encouraged but not required
to supplement the produce provided with other
sustainably grown and pure ingredients.

Disposal:

Any food that is not consumed by humans,
including trimmings and inedible portions, shall
be put to the best possible use: feed animals
before composting and compost before discarding.
Food scraps are a source of energy and fertility,
not waste products.

Commingling? I wonder, taking another forkful of cake.

Cocoa-Coconut Flip Cake

Active time: 15 minutes. Total time: 50 minutes. Serves 8.

1 cup white whole wheat flour (120 grams)
¾ cup sugar (150 grams)
2 tablespoons cocoa (10 grams)
2 teaspoons baking powder

½ teaspoon salt
½ cup coconut milk (homemade or So Delicious
          unsweetened organic coconut milk beverage)
2 tablespoons coconut spread (28 grams)
1 teaspoon vanilla

Sauce
¾ cup water (177 grams)
¾ cup brown sugar (163 grams)
1 tablespoon cocoa (5 grams)

Heat oven to 350°F. Grease an 8-inch square baking pan. In a medium bowl, stir together flour, sugar, cocoa, baking powder, and salt.

Heat coconut milk and coconut spread in a microwave-safe container such as a Pyrex measuring cup until spread melts, about one minute on high in the microwave. Stir vanilla into liquid and pour onto flour mixture. Stir until smooth, using a spatula to include any dry parts on the bottom of the bowl. More stirring is not better, though: you don't want to make the cake tough. Pour batter into the pan.

Heat water in a microwave on high until hot to the touch, about one minute. (Yes, use that same Pyrex measuring cup.) Put hot water, brown sugar, and remaining cocoa into the batter bowl. Swish to combine and to pick up remaining batter. Gently pour hot liquid over cake batter. Bake for 35 minutes or until the top is medium brown and chocolate sauce bubbles around the edges.

Put the cake pan on a wire rack to cool for about 10 minutes, then serve by cutting into pieces, flipping onto the serving plate, and topping with any chocolate sauce left in the pan.

Keep any extra covered at room temperature for about three days. To serve, cut, flip, top, and then microwave until topping goes molten again, about 30 seconds on high per serving.

HE'S GOT TO BE KIDDING

I text Charlotte: u sign crazy contract w farmer bee?!

Charlotte replies: yes so worth it. talk soon. xxoo

I continue reading Roger's contract, glad to see he's set up rules for himself as well.

RULES FOR THE FARMER

Understanding:

The Farmer thanks the Supporter for sharing the risks and rewards of agriculture, an unpredictable and challenging pursuit.

Source:

All produce provided in the weekly box shall be grown by the Farmer.

Farming method:

The Farmer will work within the natural biological cycles that are necessary for a truly sustainable farming system—a system that works in harmony with micro-organisms, soil flora and fauna, pollinators, plants, and animals. No genetically modified organisms or dangerous chemicals such as bee-killing neonicotinoids shall be used.

Neonicotinoids! That sounds like nicotine. I google it and find out that sure enough, it's a pesticide related to nicotine. It's not so bad for mammals but it paralyzes and eventually kills honey bees.

Certification:

All produce shall be United States Department of Agriculture (USDA) Certified Organic. Fertility shall come from well-nurtured, healthy soil. All processing aides will be either organic or, when

absolutely necessary, from the USDA's National
List of aides, which are generally recognized
as safe (GRAS) and contain no residues of heavy
metals or other contaminants in excess of feder-
ally approved tolerances.

Variety:

The Farmer shall make best efforts to provide
fresh produce of sufficient variety to delight the
Supporter throughout the week. All plants shall
be grown from heirloom or naturally selected
seeds, without use of any seeds from Genetically
Modified Organisms (GMOs).

Share sizes:

A full-share box shall usually contain eight
to ten items with a total average weight of eight
to ten pounds. A half-share shall usually contain
the same selection of items with a total average
weight of four to five pounds. A full share usually feeds four people in a typical household or
two active cooks.

Seasonal variation:

Farming is a dance with Nature, but as in
middle school, not every dance goes well. The
Farmer and Supporter will share the bountiful
times as well as the lean times, with the Farmer
doing his best to provide the above-specified
quantities of high-quality produce appropriate to
the season.

Duly signed and agreed on this date …

I check out agreements from other CSAs that are posted online.
Most are just a paragraph or two, talking about payment, missed
pickups, and boxes. Roger's is the most detailed by far.

But even though it feels a little, um, restrictive, I find myself
drawn to his vision. I want to be part of the dance of nature, even if
it means learning to cook.

I always love getting roasted root vegetables at the Neomonde
Café. How hard can it be to do it myself?

Roasted Roots

Active time: 15 minutes. Total time: 45 to 60 minutes.

Heat oven to 450°F. For easy cleanup, line a rimmed cookie sheet or two with parchment paper.

Scrub a mix of root vegetables, peel as needed, and cut into bite-sized pieces so they finish cooking at about the same time. Carrots and white potatoes don't need peeling. Sweet potatoes might and onions, garlic, and beets do. Heap the vegetables on the cookie sheet as you go.

Drizzle vegetables with olive oil and toss until well coated. Arrange them in a single layer and sprinkle with coarse salt. Roast until well browned but not burned, 30 to 45 minutes.

Serve hot or at room temperature. Refrigerate any extra for up to a week.

SIGNING UP

I read your contract," I tell Roger as he unloads boxes. I've come early to the market to evaluate the customers' buying patterns and unmet needs. That's what I tell myself. Charlotte thinks it's more about *my* unmet needs, but whatever.

"Yes?" he asks, standing tall and still in a way that created an island of calm in the bustling market square. The January wind has whipped red into his cheeks. "Are you with us or against us?"

Mama mia, he did– take this seriously! I pause before answering.

"I'll trust you to grow my food if you'll trust me to grow your business. Charlotte and I think optivores are your prime market."

He shudders. "What's an optivore? Somebody who eats eyeballs?"

"No, it's somebody who is trying to optimize something through their eating choices. They have a mix of reasons: health, religion, or just good old do-gooding. These days, folks want to know if something is organic, local, vegan, or vegetarian. Some want 'free' food: spray-free, sugar-free, oil-free, or gluten-free."

"So an optivore is a picky eater."

"No, not at all. If you think of them that way, they'll make you crazy. Think of them as great customers. Parents don't want to risk lowering their kids IQs by feeding them sprayed apples. Those big storms we've been having made global warming seem real for a lot of people."

"OK, I get it. Accentuate the positive." He adjusts the price sign on a crate of sweet potatoes.

"Right. You want to put your best foot forward, but the worst thing is to look like you're hiding something."

"I'm not *hiding* anything, but I value my privacy as much as my reputation. Folks already seem to like what I grow."

"Not enough folks, though. You're twelve subscriptions short of having a full winter season. If you want to do better for spring, let me bring a sign-in sheet so we can keep track of potential customers.

We can stay in touch online too. I'll put up a Facebook page for the site and make a simple website."

"I don't want to be pushy. The produce should speak for itself."

"It's not pushy to let people know how you can help them advance their own causes. We'll give them a chance to vote with their forks. If you'll let me do this, I think I can fill your spring subscription and get you set up to do better next fall."

"Deal," he says, handing me a weird silver pen. It's heavy compared to plastic gimme pens I usually use. I twist the top so I can sign the contract and a red laser beam comes out of the top, landing on his heart.

"Glad that thing wasn't loaded," he says. "Click, don't twist."

I twist the top again to turn off the laser, click to expose the pen tip, and sign both copies of the contract. The pen glides smoothly across the thick paper. Why does a farmer have such a high-tech pen?

I hand Roger his copy. He stows it in the inlaid box and shakes my hand. A burning shock of pleasure zips up my arm, as unexpected as the thrill of biting a hot pepper hidden in Super Wok's Tri-Pepper Tofu.

"The clock is ticking," he says, sliding a half-share box across the table. "Earn this by filling up my spring subscription list before March 15th."

I pick up the box and head toward the escalator, thoughts jangling around in my head. First, I'd want to delight Roger's existing customers so they'd sign up for another season. What if I gave them a recipe that would satisfy most optivores? What about an easy, thrifty stew that is gluten-free, vegan, and hearty?

Core Recipe: Cooking Dried Beans

Active time: 5 minutes. Total time: at least two hours.

1 pound dry beans (black beans, cannellini beans, navy beans,
pintos, or chickpeas) (454 grams)
1½ teaspoon salt
6 cups water
cook-in seasonings, depending on the recipe

Pick over beans, throwing out any small, wrinkled beans,
stones, or twigs. Rinse well and put in a slow cooker or a medium
pot with salt and water, then cover. Soak them for up to twelve
hours if you have time.

Stir in any cook-in seasonings to add deep flavor. Some seasonings, including bay leaves, epazote, and kombu, make the beans
easier to digest (less gassy!).

Cook beans covered on low for about seven hours in the slow
cooker. If you are cooking them on the stove, bring beans to a boil
on high, then reduce heat and cook on low until nearly tender,
about two hours for soaked beans. If you didn't soak beans, cook
them about an hour longer in the slow cooker or thirty minutes
more on the stove. Add water as needed to keep beans covered.

Cook until beans are completely tender or continue with
another recipe, such as Everybody's Happy Bean-and-Green Stew
(next page).

Everybody's Happy Bean-and-Green Stew
Active time: 10 minutes. Total time: varies. Serves 10.

1 pound cooked dried cannellini beans, cooked (previous page)

cook-in seasonings
3 bay leaves
3 garlic cloves, minced
1 yellow onion, chopped
2 teaspoons smoked paprika

1 pound mustard greens, kale, or collards (454 grams)

Cook beans and cook-in seasonings until beans are nearly tender (see above). This recipe is tasty with any type of bean, but white beans look best with the greens.

Chop greens by cutting stems into ¼-inch pieces and cutting leaves into strips about ¼ inch wide by 2 inches long. Stir greens into beans about 45 minutes before beans are completely tender. Continue cooking until beans and vegetables are tender. Remove bay leaves.

Serve hot in a bowl as soup or over baked sweet potatoes, brown rice, or quinoa. Keeps refrigerated for up to a week and frozen for at least a year.

WORK IT OUT, BABY

Use everything you want for a week," says Buck as he straps me into the vinyl and chrome device. "Everything."

His biceps ripple as he stretches my legs just below the point of pain.

"How's that?"

"More."

His thigh brushes my Lycra-clad knee. Holy cannoli, Buck was built like an oak.

"OK, that's thirty pounds. Show me."

I strain my knees apart as wide as I can, feeling the inner muscles pull and the outer muscles scream in protest. It's my first time, so I'm a little scared. Buck senses my near panic.

"Breath."

Pounding music sets a relentless rhythm as I go again, opening my legs wider each time. The salty tang of the dimly lit room fills my lungs. Mmmm, testosterone and sweat. My breasts lift. I arch my back and pull my knees closed before starting again. And whoops, again! I want to please him, to be a good girl.

"Slowly, slowly . . . That's it. Way to go," Buck urges me on, his deep voice carrying through the din. "Do two more sets of ten each while I check on that guy on the bench press. Don't forget to breath."

I watch my new personal trainer walk across the gym. Buck is mine for at least a week, while I explore the three-story health club next to the Renaissance Hotel. My anger and loneliness can't be contained anymore by the small but sufficient gym at Park & Market. The coupon for a free seven-day trial puts the Fitness Connection right in my price range.

I watch Buck walk beneath the huge banners hanging from the ceiling, each with mammoth photos of scantily clad twenty-somethings pounding themselves into shape. If the gods came down from Mount Olympus to work out, they wouldn't look any more desirable or committed.

Movement catches my eye on the balcony that overlooks the equipment room. *Kenny?!?* My already pounding heart kicks it up a notch. His dark good looks make me strain a little more, wider and wider. He's lean, masterful, all business. Rich like those Wall Street traders.

I tear my eyes away because this man staring down at me cannot be Kenny. Kenny is still in East Fishkill. This hunk is probably one of the many businessmen who spend their weeknights in the hotel. Some have weekday girlfriends in town, with the sparks starting up here at the health club or over at the Yard House. The rogues have weekend wives too.

Buck's return saves me from the shame of having looked so intimately at a stranger. In his tight tank top and clinging gym pants, my personal trainer looks like a short-haired Fabio, straight off the cover of a bodice ripper. *Look at Buck, not at The-Guy-Who-Isn't-Kenny.*

"How was that?" Buck asks. "Good?" I can barely hear him over the pounding beat of Beyoncé. Yes, Kenny, if you'd liked it, why *didn't* you put a ring on it?

"Ready for the next one," I say as Buck releases me from the machine. "More than ready."

When I get back to my apartment, I am thoroughly wrung out. I reach for my blender to whip up a smoothie. By making my own instead of dropping by the juice bar, I can also afford a matinee at the Regal. There should be some advantage to being laid off.

Use-It-or-Lose-It Green Smoothies
Active time: 4 minutes. Total time: 4 minutes. Serves 2.

1 tablespoon dried coconut
1 cup water
2 medium bananas
10 ounces frozen blueberries (280 grams)
about 4 cups roughly chopped greens (spinach, arugula, chickweed, Swiss chard, mustard, collards)

Put dried coconut and water into a blender and process on high while you peel bananas and cut them into one-inch slices. Put banana slices and blueberries into blender and process until smooth.

Tear up greens into hand-sized pieces, saving large stems on Swiss chard, mustard, or collards for another recipe. Put leaves into the blender. Process until high (or on the "smoothie" setting if your blender has one) until mixture is smooth. If mixture doesn't blend, stop the blender and poke greens down with a spatula, then try again.

Drink cold. Refrigerate any extra, which will thicken to become almost like a pudding as it chills.

Brush your teeth so they don't stain and so you don't scare people with your blue chompers.

DOG EAT DOG

It's nearly noon on the third Saturday of January. Roger asks me to mind the stand while he takes some unsold produce over to Nicole at the Help the Hungry booth. Just after he leaves, two women and their herd come up to the table. Each has an infant in a stroller. Five other children swarm around them so it's hard to say who belongs to whom.

They don't look like the other customers. I'm used to seeing kids wearing hand-me-downs, but not adults. The cut of the two friends' jackets say thrift shop or even Goodwill. They look thin in a hungry way, not with the self-assured self-deprivation of supermodels.

"I'm Sally Johnson and this is Ruth Carter," says one of the moms. Her blonde hair has expensive-looking streaks, but I bet they're from the sun, not foils. They both wear their hair long, one in braids and one in a ponytail. If I don't get a real job soon, I'm going to have to give up appointments at Salon Blu myself. Six-dollar Super Cuts may be in my future, but not home-hacked bangs. I already did my first self-pedicure in years last night, although the only people likely to see my naked toes will have their minds on Zumba.

I check off their names and exchange boxes. "What do you tell the nice lady?" Sally prompts the eight-year-old who reaches eagerly for the box.

"Thank you, Ma'am," he said shyly, looking down at the table.

"Tell Roger we'll settle up soon," Ruth said.

"Will do," I reply even though I'm not sure what she means. The whole point of a CSA is that the farmer gets the money in advance. She must be talking about something else.

Roger is walking back toward me finally. Nicole looks after him with a look that says she wishes he'd stay. She's barely half his age, like Harrison Ford's girlfriend in that movie last week. Even in bright sunlight, Nicole's skin is flawless. What on earth made me crouch over my toes with such concentration last night, trying to

get a twenty-dollar look from a two-dollar bottle of polish? Kenny is
gone. Buck's interest in my heart is strictly aerobic. Roger must see
me as an employee.

I wrap my hands around my thermos for warmth and look
through the windows into Starbucks, where a dozen or so people
are warm, dry, and about to be fully caffeinated. Maybe Roger even
sees me as a hardship case, as somebody he's taken on to please
Charlotte.

Charlotte picks up her box. Soon, every name is checked off
the list. All but two of the current subscribers said they wanted to
receive newsletters with recipes and previews of what would be in
their boxes. I proudly show Roger this list as we start closing down
the booth for the day.

He picks up the clipboard. "Ten new people already signed up
for our newsletter?"

"No, nine. I always have 'Cindy Lou Bailey' sign up so no one
has to be first."

"And everyone wants *to live the life of Cindy Lou, do the things
Cindy Lou would do?*"

"Exactly. Cindy Lou makes people comfortable. That's why
I'm handing out this recipe for greens with peanut sauce. Charlotte
swears it will make everyone who tries it feel like a great cook, even
optivores. Kids will eat cardboard if you put peanut butter on it."

Steamed Collards with Peanut-Lime Sauce

Active time: 20 minutes. Total time: 20 minutes. Serves .

2 garlic cloves
1 pound fresh collards (454 grams)
1 teaspoon grated fresh ginger
¼ cup peanut butter (64 grams)
2 tablespoons soy sauce
1 tablespoon lime juice
⅛ teaspoon chipotle

Mince garlic and put into a small bowl. Rinse collards well.

Set up a steamer by putting about an inch of water in a large pot, adding a steamer basket, and covering the pot. Heat steamer over high heat until water starts to boil, then turn temperature down to low so water barely boils.

Cut or tear collard leaves away from the center stems. Cut off the bottom of each stem and compost it, then cut remaining stems into quarter-inch lengths. Add stems to steamer basket and cook for about 4 minutes.

Cut collard leaves into ribbons about 2 x ¼ inches across. Put collard leaves on top of stems in the steamer and cook until tender, about 5 minutes.

Add remaining ingredients to bowl with garlic and stir to mix. When collards are tender, transfer them to a serving bowl, top with lime-peanut sauce, and stir to mix.

Serve hot or at room temperature, either as a side or tossed with cooked udon noodles as a main dish. Refrigerate any extra and reheat briefly before serving.

GREEN-EYED MONSTER

The next Saturday, Charlotte and I get to the market early to check out the other booths. We're brainstorming about a new look for Roger's booth, one more appealing than stacks of boxes on a bare table. Most other farms have some sort of display: a banner with their farm name or a chalk board listing the day's specials in bright colors.

"Your best props are in the boxes," she says. "Heap up some winter squash and put the bok choy in a basket, where people can see how pretty it is. Quit saying you are a charity case. That man needs you." She gives me a hug, then we walk back to the Bee's Knees stand.

"Morning, ladies," drawls Roger. The early morning light catches the stubble on his unshaven chin.

"Morning, Sir," we chime, then look at each other and laugh. Charlotte says she's got a million chores to run. She'll drop her box now and pick it up after she hits the pharmacy and checks out the dress sale at Monkee's.

I drop my box too, then join Roger behind the table. It's more research, I tell myself, not just a chance to stand closer to the man whom I'd secretly painted my toenails for. The image of his flannel cuff opening up to show a glimpse of strong wrist and forearm made me want to roll that cuff up further, to kiss . . . .

Something Roger says cuts through my reverie. "What?" I ask.

"I said, would you please watch the boxes for a minute while I go see Nicole? Just check people's names off on this list as they come by. Tell them we've got the first of the baby bok choy this week."

"Sure, fine." I watch him stride across the green to the Help the Hungry donation table. That denim jacket might not keep his ass warm, but I'm glad it doesn't block the view.

Three families come by to swap empty boxes for full ones. I feel like a magician when I open the lids. Even the kids get excited.

"Purple carrots!"

"Fennel!"

And even, "Arugula!"

I never thought I'd live to hear a four-year-old say, "Mommy, look, more 'pinach!"

Everyone seems delighted to see the bok choy, ultra fresh with firm white stems and broad, pale green leaves. The leaves join at the base like lettuce or celery. They form a bundle the size of Roger's hand (there's that image again!), far younger than you can find in the store.

A couple stops by to ask about joining the CSA. The beads in his dreads and in her hand-knit sweater glint in the sun. I capture the woman's name and email address on the sign-in sheet, promising to send information on the spring subscription.

I glance over at Roger and Nicole, wondering just what kind of donation she's angling for today. She leans close to him with her hand gripping his arm. Her rustic knit sweater stretches across large breasts as she tucks a wavy blonde lock behind her ear. If Botticelli came back from the dead to paint angelic volunteers, he might ask Nicole to be his model.

Roger laughs at something Nicole says. I feel a hot stab of jealously. *Calm down, Sophia. He's your client, not your boyfriend.*

I turn away to watch Lucy at Loco Local Sandwiches work the grill. I feel as hot and green as whatever that is she's flipping with her tongs.

Grilled Baby Bok Choy

Active time: 5 minutes. Total time: 14 minutes. Serves 2.

1 tablespoon olive oil
1 clove garlic
2 small heads bok choy (also called pak choi)
salt to taste

Mince garlic and heat with olive oil until fragrant in a metal container on the grill (or microwave on high for 40 seconds in a microwave-safe bowl).

Rinse bok choy well, cut crossways where leaves join the stalks, and then cut stem section in half top to bottom. (Save leaves for salad or a scramble.) Rinse stems again, gently pulling apart to swish away any soil lodged between them. Pat dry and rub with olive oil. Save the minced garlic and any extra oil for another recipe.

Turn gas grill on medium. Grill bok-choy halves curved-sided down for about 4 minutes, then flip and grill flat-side down for another 4 minutes.

Serve hot or warm, salted to taste.

BUTLER SHUTTLER

Hey," says Blondie as the elevator doors open on my floor, using the soft Southern greeting. "Looks like we're both going to the market." It's that pretty plump woman again. "Are you going over on the Butler Shuttler?"

"The what?" I'm dazzled by her full makeup and aggressively festive snowman sweater. Her snowflake earrings jingle. Her optimistic energy reminds me of campaign volunteers taking my walk lists for the first canvas right after Labor Day, before they get the first door slammed in their faces.

"Oh, that's what we all call it now that Mr. Simms has taken it over. He's the butler, ex-butler really. And the *Shuttler* is that cute little twelve-seater that should be waiting for us right out front. It goes from this side of Midtown across the street and all around the mall. I'm Jo Lynn Jackson, probably your upstairs neighbor."

Sure enough, when we reach the lobby I can see what looks like a stretch golf cart waiting, a portly yet dignified man in full security regalia in the driver's seat. He's wearing a stiff brimmed hat and plenty of badges, and holds a squawking walkie-talkie a bit away from his body, as if to keep the rabble from disturbing his dignified calm. I stow my car keys. Mr. Simms uses Masterpiece Theatre tones to recommend that we put our boxes in the back of the little bus, then tells the dispatcher he's on the way.

We zip across Six Forks Road. I admire the cluster of new high rises on this side of the Beltline. Their glass panels reflect and frame the sky, seeming natural and artificial at the same time.

Minutes later, I'm dodging toddlers on the town square. Roger and Nicole seem to having a debate at the Help the Hungry booth, but stop abruptly as Jo Lynn sings out a cheerful "Good morning, y'all!"

I start hanging up the new banner. Getting the first clip in is easy, but the wind keeps jerking it out of my hands. I curse under my breath and try again.

"Here, let me get that for you, Sugar." Roger is suddenly behind me, close, reaching up over my head to fasten the banner to the booth frame. I turn to look up at him, brushing my check against the soft flannel covering his arm. I'm pinned between him and the table for a too-short moment.

"There, that's better. Let's see what you got."

The banner says *Bee's Knees Farm* in big green letters. Cartoon bees based on the one on Roger's contract fly around the banner with speech bubbles that announce *organic! local! fresh!*

Roger steps back to survey the booth, a grin spreading across his face. "Bodacious! That banner makes us look like we're in the big league. Love the bees."

He spots the bee decal I've added to the newsletter clipboard. With a laugh of delight, he lifts me off my feet and spins me around in a big bear hug. Jason and Haruka at the Edible Earthscapes booth next door see our silliness and applaud.

"So you're the famous Cindy Lou, begging for my newsletter again!" Roger says, lips close to my ear.

"I'm surely not *Sugar*."

"No, you're much more interesting than that. Darker, smoother. More Southern and probably more nutritious, too. I'm going to call you *Sorghum*."

Core Recipe: Flaxseed Egg
Active time: 1 minute. Total time: 2 minutes. Makes 1 "egg."

1 tablespoon finely ground flaxseed (14 grams)
3 tablespoons water (see variations below)

Heat flaxseed and water in a microwave-safe bowl on high for about 40 seconds, then stir with a fork to develop eggy texture. Let cool to room temperature before using if main recipe uses baking powder, baking soda, or would otherwise be affected by a warm "egg."

Variations: Use as little as one tablespoon water to get binding power without extra moisture. Microwave for about 30 seconds if using 2 tablespoons water or about 20 seconds for 1 tablespoon. Use other liquids to intensify the flavor of the main recipe, such as apple juice or broth. If you don't want to use a microwave, just pour boiling liquid over the flaxseed, wait a few seconds, and stir.

Banana Pancakes with Sorghum

Active time: 20 minutes. Total time: 20 minutes. Makes 12 pancakes.

1 flaxseed "egg" (see above)
¼ teaspoon canola oil
2 tablespoons Earth Balance organic coconut spread (28 grams)
1½ cup water
1 cup white whole wheat flour (120 grams)
1 tablespoon sugar
1½ teaspoons baking powder
½ teaspoon salt
zest of one lemon or orange
1 banana
½ cup sorghum for topping (see notes)

Make flaxseed egg. Spread oil on a flat griddle or skillet with your fingers. Heat griddle to medium high or 370°F.

Put coconut spread in a microwave safe container and heat on high until melted, about 15 seconds. Stir in flaxseed egg and water.

In a medium bowl, stir flour, sugar, baking powder, and salt with a fork to mix.

Zest lemon over the flour mixture, then stir again. Stir wet ingredients into dry ingredients. Cut banana into quarters lengthwise, then cut crossways into ½-inch sections. Stir banana into batter.

Spoon or ladle batter onto hot griddle. Cook until bubbles stop rising in the pancakes and bottoms turn golden, about 3 minutes. Use a spatula to flip each pancake and continue cooking until brown on both sides, about a minute more.

Heat sorghum in a microwave-safe container on medium. Stir and pour over hot pancakes. Serve immediately.

Don't have sorghum? Put it on your grocery list and use maple syrup or honey until you get some.

WHAT GOES WHERE

"Charlotte, you've got to help me!" I beg when she comes by the next Sunday. She and her boyfriend Bill went to Wilmington for the weekend, so I'd picked up her box again. "What do you do with all this stuff? I've been making smoothies like crazy for a month, but I can't keep up."

"Well, you don't keep the Swiss chard in a vase, for one thing."

I'd arranged the tropical-looking leaves in a crystal vase to show off the red, yellow, and hot-pink stems. "That's *Swiss* chard? It looks like Hawaiian chard! Tarzan must eat leaves like this!"

"Swiss it is. Wrap it in a damp paper towel and put it in the fridge. It keeps for a few days, so I usually start by eating the salad mix and lettuce first. Here, I'll show you my system. Do you have any plastic bags from the grocery store? And paper towels?"

"Sure, here you go."

She takes a knife down from the magnet strip behind my cutting board and cuts the leaves off the beets and carrots.

"Wait! Why are you doing that? They're so pretty!"

"Fresh is better than pretty," she said, tucking the leaves into bags with a damp paper towel each. "The roots will last a lot longer if the leaves aren't sucking the moisture out of them."

Charlotte open the door of my refrigerator and sighs. "You do know you're supposed to eat this stuff, not save it for posterity."

"I am. Eating it and eating it *and eating it*! But a new box comes every week."

"The trick is to stow the food you will eat last in the back, so you can just start grazing from the front every week. Put in the really sturdy greens like collards and kale first; then Swiss chard, beet greens, and mustard. Look how pretty this Buttercrunch lettuce looks in front, like a big flower."

"What about the roots?"

"Put beets, carrots, and turnips in bags in the fridge. But potatoes, onions, and garlic want a cool, dark spot." She opens the pantry door next the fridge. "A rolling wire rack would fit here and make it easy to keep clean. Get one with at least two shelves so you can keep potatoes and onions separate. They encourage each other to sprout."

I wipe the counter clean, stow the box in the pantry for next week, and pour us each a glass of wine. Charlotte tells me about the trends she spotted at the coast while she bustles around my kitchen.

"Wilmington landed another TV show and the chefs have finally figured out that the Beautiful People want fresh, not fried, and local, local, local. The farmers should get Emmys for keeping up. Did you know that Roger is going to plant fresh baby ginger this spring?"

"Ginger! I can make Chard Hawaii!"

Charlotte rolls her eyes, then takes another sip and leans forward. "Speaking of fresh, what about Roger? I'd subscribe to him even if he didn't have such great chard."

"Roger! Not my type at all, and not yours either. He's all flannel shirt and red clay." I try to say it like I mean it. I'm not ready to talk about the unexpected pull I'm feeling.

"I don't know, Sophia. If I weren't dating Bill, I'd definitely be angling for a farm tour."

"I am getting a tour on Tuesday, but it's strictly business. Roger is showing me around so I can get pictures for Facebook and a feel for what I'm selling."

"Lucky you! Listen, grab us a couple of old shirts and I'll show you how to make pickles."

"Pickled old shirts?"

"Don't be daft! The shirts will keep us from looking like we've killed a beet in cold blood."

Hot-Pink Refrigerator Pickles

Active time: 10 minutes. Total time: 1 hour. Yield: 2 cups.

1 clove garlic
2 medium turnips
1 small daikon
1 medium beet
2 tablespoons salt (most of this is rinsed off)
¼ cup brown rice vinegar
¼ teaspoon ground chipotle or cayenne
few sprigs fresh fennel or dill, chopped (optional)

Slice garlic and put into a glass or ceramic container big enough to hold the finished pickles and set aside.

Put a colander on a plate or bowl to catch vegetable juice. Trim and peel turnips, daikon, and beet and cut into thin slices.

Charlotte usually cuts the slices into strips or shapes. When she's at home, she uses a small star-shaped metal cookie cutter with sharp edges on the tender daikon and turnip slices, saving the stars and the outline of the stars.

Sprinkle vegetables with one tablespoon salt, toss, and sprinkle with remaining salt. Every few minutes for about 10 minutes, toss and gently squeeze salted vegetables. Salt draws liquid out of the vegetables, which helps them absorb vinegar later and become crisp.

When vegetables become a bit limp, rinse them under cold water, drain, and add to garlic in the glass container. Stir vinegar and chipotle together and pour over vegetables. Add fennel if using. Stir or toss to coat vegetables with vinegar, toss again about 5 minutes later, and then refrigerate until well chilled, about 40 minutes.

Serve cold. Keeps for weeks in the refrigerator if stirred occassionally.

FERME ORNÉE

I feel like I am driving a time machine, going back into the pioneering past. In less than an hour, I drive from the high-rises in Midtown, around the Beltline, and out Highway 64. Fast-food joints give way to corner gas stations with signs for bait and old-timey sodas. The long, flat bridge across the narrows of Jordan Lake is the only sign of human intervention. No motor boats or swimmers disturb the ducks bobbing for their dinners near the shore.

Past the bridge, the rounded hills of North Carolina's Piedmont has farms or trees instead of shopping centers and billboards. Flicka's GPS app tells me to turn down a two-lane paved road and drive for two miles.

"You have arrived at your destination," says Flicka. I see an unpaved road, practically a set of tire tracks, leading away from a mailbox on a post near the edge of the pavement. The cartoon bee from the contract does a little jig on the mailbox over the words *Bee's Knees Farm*. I'm so happy to not be lost that I do a little seat jig too.

My Prius bounces through sparse woods of bare trees and green pines. About a quarter mile down the road, the trail goes up through a twiggy tunnel, around a bend, and out onto gently rolling fields. A white two-story farmhouse nestles between two brick chimneys, with stubbly fields on the left and low green crops on the right. A barn sits behind the house, the same dusty red as the brick. Roger waves from the broad, wrap-around porch, then gestures toward a parking area.

"Howdy, Sorghum," he says as I got out of the car.

"It's gorgeous, like a Southern version of a Courier and Ives print! I should have worn a calico bonnet."

He looks me up and down, his gaze heating me up from inside my Italian leather boots to just under my fedora. I wish my sunglasses were even bigger, big enough to hide my red cheeks.

"Gorgeous, yes," he says, not looking at the farm. "As Stephen Switzer wrote, 'By mixing the useful and profitable parts of Gard'ning with the Pleasurable … My Designs are thereby vastly enlarg'd and both Profit and Pleasure may be agreeably mix'd together.'"

He pauses. I think about my favorite ways of mixing profit and pleasure. A Carolina warbler trills.

Roger shakes his head as if to clear it and looks away. "But we're not old fashioned, more Common Threads than calico. Let me show you around, at least as far we can go with you wearing those boots."

I jump as he whistles sharply. Three dogs surge from behind the house. For a moment the world is all black, grey, and white fur with broad pink tongues and toothy smiles. Roger reaches down to rub them, then whistles a different trill. They scramble to sit in front of him, gazing up with love and hope.

"They're almost blue!"

"Yes, these sisters are Blue Merle border collies: June, Patsy, and Dolly. Great herders and smarter than most of my bosses. I couldn't run the farm without them."

"I'm mostly a cat person, but some of my best friends have been dogs."

"Best friends and old boyfriends, I bet you mean." Roger grins wickedly. "Let's start with the greens."

As we near to the fields, I recognize plants from my CSA box. There's rainbow chard, growing in rows instead of on the big tropical vines I'd imagined.

"Thomas Jefferson might have called this place a *Ferme Ornée*."

"Fair mornay?"

"Yes, French for *decorated farm*. It's a working farm too, like Monticello or Polyface. A little thought lends beauty to utility."

"Is that Jefferson too? Or Shakespeare?"

"Strictly Branch."

Roger pulls on a cluster of dark red leaves in a neighboring row. I laugh as a beet pops out from under the dirt.

"This one's a Chioggia, an Italian heirloom just like you," he says, cutting through the dark globe with his pocket knife. *Wow o wow!* Rings within rings inside, dark beet-purple alternating with white. "I sell all I can grow. Kids love the surprise and cooks love the flavor."

"I love the looks. Let me get a picture for your newsletter," I said, pulling out Flicka.

"Shoot the farm, not me," he says, turning away abruptly. I mute Flicka and take a few shots of him from behind with the rows of vegetables curving across the field and up toward the river. He looks so darned rugged, so sure of his place. I feel like a tween who's just snapped Justin Bieber.

In the next field, he breaks off the end of a delicate vine and hands it to me.

"Taste it."

"Flower and all?"

"We get about eight dollars a pound for the tips and young pods of these Australian peas. They add nitrogen, too. In a few weeks, we'll mow the peas down and plant tomatoes."

"So they're both crop and fertilizer!"

He nods with approval. "You've got a feel for this farming thing. Most cityfolk don't put together how one plant can feed them and the soil too. Tell me, did you have a garden when you were a kid?"

Suddenly the memories of the garden I'd tended with the focus only an eight-year-old can have came flooding back to me. "Yes! I grew marigolds and saved the seeds. My father showed me how to hand-pollinate sweet peas, just like Mendel. We picked out which traits we wanted for the next year's flowers, at least for a few years."

"Was he a geneticist?"

"No, but Papà loved reading about science and trying it out at home. If he hadn't left Mamma when I was ten, I might have gone into biology."

We walk back to the house. After a few minutes, Roger says, "Come again next Friday when the crew packs the boxes."

I nod, then stumble as my heel sinks into a soft spot. Roger catches my elbow so I don't plant myself in the collards.

"Come the Friday after next instead. First I want to take you shopping for real boots. We'll go Saturday after market."

When I get home, I find a gift bag with a quart jar of what looks like flour and a note from Charlotte. *Please test my Good Baking Mix. I think I've found a way for non-cooks to make great biscuits! xxoo C*

Non-cooks, I think. Thanks so much. But I limp inside to try it.

Core Recipe: Good Baking Mix

Active time: 10 minutes. Total time: 10 minutes. Makes about 4 cups, enough for 2 dozen biscuits.

2 cups all-purpose, unbleached flour (240 grams)
1 cup white whole wheat flour (120 grams)
¼ cup wheat germ, untoasted (32 grams)
2 tablespoons baking powder
1¼ teaspoon salt
½ cup Earth Balance organic coconut spread (4 ounces or 114 grams)

Put dry ingredients in a food processor fitted with a cutting blade and pulse a few times to combine.

Drop coconut spread by the spoonful into the food processor, then pulse until mixture resembles coarse sand.

Use immediately or refrigerate in a tightly sealed container for up to one month.

Variation: If you don't like the taste of coconut or just prefer buttery-tasting biscuits, use chickpea flour instead of wheatgerm and Earth Balance soy-free natural buttery spread instead of coconut spread.

PAYING ATTENTION

As I put together a website for the Bee's Knees Farm, I notice how many more pictures than notes I have. Usually when I work with politicians, they say so much in such perfect sound-bite units that my hand aches from writing at the end of a session.

Even Kenny talked at least twice as much as Roger does. Kenny made me laugh talking about his crazy schemes. Why did I find the farmer so much more interesting?

I look back through my notes. A few words keep popping out. *Cycle. Years. Generations. Future.*

He's thinking long-term, not just about the next poll or next election. Even though he doesn't have kids, he's farming like he'll be around forever — or another farmer he cares about will be.

As I think back to what I didn't write down, something else strikes me: Roger talked about farming because I asked him to. And he asked questions about me, questions related to what I'd said or done, not some speed-dating checklist. We'd had an actual conversation instead of performing two competing monologues.

Or one monologue with an admiring audience, as it had so often been with Kenny.

I try Charlotte's biscuit recipe with the fancy variation that almost makes them look like classic rolled and cut-out biscuits. She says that after dropping globs of rough biscuit dough onto a cooking sheet, just dampen your hands and pat each biscuit smooth.

Funny how a few soft pats in the right places can make all the difference.

Good Mix Biscuits

Active time: 3 minutes. Total time: 12 minutes. Makes 6 biscuits, multiplies well.
1 cup Good Baking Mix (120 grams) (page 44)
⅓ cup of water

Heat oven or convection toas¹ter-oven to 450°F. In a medium bowl, stir mix and water together until just wet. Stirring more will make the biscuits tough.

Use a soup spoon to drop dough onto an ungreased cookie sheet or cake pan. Bake for 8 to 10 minutes, until golden brown.

Serve within 15 minutes if possible. Biscuits keep for a day or two covered at room temperature.

YOU SAY PO-TAY-TO, I SAY PO-TAH-TO

My oh my, I would totally subscribe to *that*," Charlotte says, giggling as she looks at my proposed website for Bee's Knees Farm. "And I mean the stud, not the spuds."

"He *is* mighty photogenic. Do you think that's the right picture for the home page?" I start up the slide show of the keeper shots from my trip to the farm. It's odd to see it come to life on an iPad propped up between two tiny espresso cups on my granite kitchen island. I take a big bite of muffin while I wait for Charlotte's response.

The farm house, waving rows of greens, the fancy beets in Roger's hand, a close up of Roger smiling, several long shots of him under the blue Carolina skies, and finally an accidental shot taken as I stumbled, showing him looking at me with amusement and concern.

"Mmm, mmm, mmm! Look at that strong jaw and those green, green eyes." Charlotte squeezed my arm while staring at my iPad. "He could pose for a Patagonia ad. You've got the right picture for the home page, but I can see why you would want to keep them all."

He did look even better in the photographs than in person. Maybe that was because I can relax now and drink him in. No worries about being caught staring.

Charlotte picks up the other half of her muffin. "I'm glad to see you finally going after something fun. And I don't just mean the project."

Sweet Potato Muffins

Active time: 20 minutes. Total time: 45 minutes. 12 muffins.

1 cup cooked, mashed sweet potato (200 grams)
¼ cup canola oil
2 teaspoons grated fresh ginger
1 orange (zest and juice)
enough water to stretch orange juice to 1¼ cups
2½ cup white whole wheat flour (300 grams)
2 tablespoons finely ground flaxseed (14 grams)
2 teaspoons baking powder
½ teaspoon baking soda
¼ teaspoon salt
¾ cup packed brown sugar (165 grams)
shortening or paper cupcake liners

Heat oven to 375°F. Lightly grease a twelve-cup muffin pan or use paper liners.

In a medium bowl, stir together sweet potato, oil, ginger, and orange zest. Juice orange, then add water to juice to make 1¼ cups liquid. Stir into sweet-potato mixture.

Stir flour, flaxseed, baking powder, baking soda, and salt in a large bowl with a fork or whisk until well blended. Stir in brown sugar.

Stir wet ingredients into dry ones just until well combined, with no dry flour lurking at the bottom of the bowl.

Divide batter evenly in the muffin cups and bake for 20 to 25 minutes, until a toothpick inserted into the center of a muffin comes out clean. Remove from muffin tin and cool individual muffins on a wire rack for at least 5 minutes. Cool thoroughly then store in a sealed container at room temperature for up to four days or wrap well and freeze.

MADE IT!

I check my email for the third time in a half hour. Today is the deadline for filling up the Bee's Knees spring list and we're still two full subscriptions short. It was harder to get people to commit to three months of produce than to get them to vote!

Mamma's sent me a link to an article about *Asheville's Most Eligible Bachelors*. I guess that's better than the feature on *Health Insurance for Spinsters* she sent yesterday. I click the trash icon with a little more force than is strictly necessary.

I check our Facebook page and do a little dance of joy. Someone's posted a link to a story about CSAs in today's *News and Observer*. Excellent! The story lists a dozen farms with CSAs in the Triangle. It's alphabetical, so Bee's Knees Farm comes first.

I take the stairs down to my mailbox to get my paper, too eager to wait for the elevator. *Yes!* It's the feature story in the Living section. A big photo showing one of our boxes looks like one of those portraits of Bounty at the art museum. The Buttercrunch lettuce is front and center among asparagus, strawberries, green garlic, rainbow chard, and a bouquet of herbs.

I check my email again. Someone has posted the story to the Carolina Farm Stewardship's listserv. Mary Beth Hardison copies me on an email sent to forty or so friends, linking to the article and saying how much she loves getting Roger's produce every week. She mentions the recipe I gave out for stir-fried pea shoots.

Then one email asks for a half-subscription, another for a full. I post the article on our website and check Facebook again. Five customers add their testimonials to the link about the story.

Flicka sounds a hunting ringtone I haven't heard in a long time. It's the one I use for elected officials. I see the campaign portrait of one of my favorite city councilors.

"I was wondering what you'd been up to, Sophia," he says. "Is it too late to get a subscription? A small one, just for me and my wife?"

I set up his subscription, then call Charlotte.

"Girl, it's time to celebrate! Meet me at Bruegger's in thirty?"

I take off my sweats and reach for my jeans. A glance in the mirror shows how boringly practical my panties look. On the other hand, my waistline is coming back. My jeans are so loose that I add a belt. It cinches in two holes tighter than it had at Christmas.

I get two coffees and two bagels: sundried tomato for me and the new Morning Glory with apple, carrots, and sunflower seeds for Charlotte. She always wants the new new.

Our order is ready just as Charlotte comes through the door. She hands me the story she's cut out of her paper and gives me a hug.

"Here's a copy for your scrapbook."

"Thanks! I'll laminate mine and post it at the booth."

We're nearly done with our bagels when Charlotte tells me how much Bill had enjoyed the new lacy thong she bought at Target last week.

"I went on a spring splurge last week. Bill loves it when I give him a fashion show. I got some cute boyshorts too."

I push the last quarter of my bagel away. "Do you have time to help me pick some out? Maybe there's a fashion show in Roger's future too."

"Whoo-hoo, girlfriend! I knew you were going to let him plow your field!"

"Peg at Eden Farms tells me there's still a risk of frost for a few weeks. But it can't hurt to get our equipment ready."

I call Mr. Simms to take us across the street to the Target on the lower level.

Stir-Fried Pea Shoots with Ginger and Garlic

Active time: 10 minutes. Total time: 12 minutes. Serves 2 as a main dish or 4 as a side.

3 garlic cloves
½ pound pea shoots (225 grams)
1½ teaspoons minced ginger
1 teaspoon peanut or canola oil
1 whole dried red pepper
1 tablespoon soy sauce

Mince garlic and set aside. Pick over pea shoots, removing any yellowed or bruised parts. If you spot a few pea flowers, reserve one as garnish for each person. Rinse pea shoots well in three changes of water, then spin dry in a salad spinner. Usually the shoots will be less than 4 inches long and won't need any other preparation, but if you have very long ones, cut them into sections.

Put pea shoots on a clean towel to dry a little more. Rinse pea flowers and set aside.

Mince ginger and measure remaining ingredients.

Heat a wok following the manufacturer's instructions. (I turn my electric wok up to high.) Pour oil down side of the wok. Add garlic, ginger, and red pepper. Stir and cook until fragrant and pepper puffs up, about 20 seconds. Add pea shoots, stirring them constantly as they wilt, for about 2 minutes.

Pour soy sauce into wok down the side and immediately cover wok. Turn heat to low and let pea shoots steam for about 2 minutes. Serve at once as a side dish or tossed with hot udon noodles for a main dish, topped with raw pea flowers.

DAS BOOT

Roger treats me to a quick lunch from the Loco Local Sandwich booth just before it shuts down. We load up Roger's truck and head over to the REI.

I have never been in the outdoor-gear store before, but am pleased to see it's not a jock jungle like Dick's or one of the other no-pain-no-gain warehouses.

We walk up wide wood stairs to the second floor, then head over to the boots. Many of the displays have signs announcing REI's big spring sale. I'm relieved, thinking about how I need to stretch my savings until I get another paycheck. When I look at the prices, though, I gasp.

"These cost as much as Manolos!"

"Man-who-lows? Couldn't say." Roger says, unmoved by the price tag. "Think of it as an investment. Good boots last about ten years. With the right socks and insoles, they'll let you hike places you can never go in your show boots. Hiking is pretty much free once you get there."

"But $300!"

"What's it worth to you to not twist your pretty ankle?" He holds up a pair of boots from the sale table. They're pretty cute, not the clunky things I'd imagined. Light, too, mostly waterproof fabric in silver and deep turquoise.

When I slide off my boots, Roger snorts at my thin knee-highs.

"Bad boots, bad socks. I bet your feet hurt at night."

"It's the price of beauty."

"Beauty doesn't have a face that says *my feet hurt*. Let me get you some real socks." Roger stands up as a clerk approaches. He looks like a guy who works at REI for the employee discount.

"Hey, Roger. Sorry it's taken me so long to get over to you. Folks are swarming this sale."

"No worries, Frank. Sophia, Frank is one of the Raleigh Outing Club's most active hiking leaders. Let him measure your feet while I get you some real socks."

"I know my shoe size!"

"Yes, but as Lenin said, 'Doveryai, no proveryai.' Trust yet verify. You know your styling size, not your walking size."

Frank measures my feet, then brings back three boxes of boots, including a pair of Merrill's someone had just returned. "I can give you a good deal on these if they fit. They'll give you a lot of boot for the buck." A woman surrounded by a stack of boxes whoo-hoos for more. Frank dashes off to grab boxes to help her.

"I'll show you how to lace up boots," Roger says as he kneels before me and slides my knee-high down my right calf. His hands brush my leg more than strictly necessary, warming me despite the cool store air.

He covers my bare foot with a thick sock that has the name Smart Wool woven into the insteps. Even socks have brains these days.

"Does it hurt here?" he asks, rubbing my instep with his thumb. "Or here?" He pulls gently on my toes. I nod, unwilling to speak in case my voice reveals just how much I want him to keep rubbing.

"Bad shoes are a misery that can be avoided. It's a shame to hurt such pretty feet." He slides on the boot, then braces my foot on his thigh while he laces them up. "Catch the laces in the first two hooks, then twist the laces together three times before you put them in the top hooks. That will keep them from working loose while you're walking the back forty."

He repeats the process with my left foot, but this time looking deep into my eyes as he smoothes the sock across my instep and up my ankle. My mouth goes dry. Maybe it's time to shop for a tent.

"Walk down the aisle and back to see how they feel."

I stand up and sway, unused to having my heel and toes on the same level when I'm not barefoot. The sturdy boots connect me with the floor in a way that suddenly seems secure. They hold my ankles firmly. I lift my foot too high with the first tentative step.

Lighter than they look and so comfortable! I adjust my gate and am soon swaggering up and down the aisle, a big grin on my face.

"Wait 'til we get you those insoles," Roger says. "You'll be farm-ready."

"I'm dessert-ready now. Let's have coffee and something sweet at my place while you look at the new website."

Roger squeezes my arm as we head down to the cashier, past posters of rock climbers and snow-covered peaks. I shiver with anticipation.

Core Recipe: Slightly Sweet Dough

Active time: 8 minutes. Total time: about 2 hours and 20 minutes.

2 cups all-purpose flour (240 grams)
1 cup white whole wheat flour (120 grams)
¼ cup wheat germ (32 grams)
2¼ teaspoon yeast (one packet)
1 teaspoon salt
2 tablespoons honey or sorghum
1⅓ cup warm water (about 115°F)
extra flour for rolling out dough

Put all ingredients in a bread machine and mix on the dough setting. If you'd rather, knead for about 8 minutes until silky by hand or with a stand mixer fitted with the dough hook. Let rise until doubled, about two hours.

At this point, you can refrigerate dough for up to two weeks in a lightly covered bowl if you don't want to use it right away. Take dough out of refrigerator about 30 minutes before filling and baking. Use dough to make Apple-Raisin Pockets (page 58).

PRIVACY

We take the Shuttler over to Park & Market, Roger carrying my produce box while I clutch the REI bag with my new boots, two pairs of Smart Wool socks, and neon-green insoles, which follow the curves of my arches nearly as well as Roger's thumb did.

We watch the elevator light blink blink blink from the penthouse to the lobby. I'm suddenly nervous. What if he doesn't like my design for his website? What will he think of my apartment?

The elevator travels right past us, down to the grocery store on the level below. When the doors finally open, we see one of the building Lotharios playfully putting a bunch of bananas in the grocery bag of a Midtown Mama. They giggle as we step into the elevator. They get off on separate floors, *for now*, as Roger and I ride up one more floor in highly charged silence. I wish I had a banana.

"Home sweet home," I say, unlocking my apartment door and stepping inside. Roger follows me, then walks straight over to the huge windows.

"The market square looks so small from up here," he says. "Small and green."

"Yes, that Astroturf was a good investment. Let me put these things away while you take a first look at the website, then we'll talk."

My heart gives a little flutter when he sits on the loveseat instead of on one of the bar stools around the granite-topped island. What luck, he's sitting on the side where I'd long hoped a lover would sit, not on the side where I've spent so much time drinking tea and reading reports and romances. I brush my iPad with a trembling finger so it shows my proposal for the Bee's Knees Farm homepage. His face lights up as he sees the pictures of the lush rows of greens. From a distance, the rows look pretty much alike, then close-ups show the personalities of various crops: tropical rainbow chard, darkly mysterious beet greens, and twining pea vines. I'm putting up my own weekly share, thinking of the photographic possibilities, when he laughs and points. I head to the love seat to see what he's looking at.

"I didn't know anyone could take a nude picture of bok choy, but look at this!"

A pair of baby bok choy lean against each other, two tender leaves just touching. They're resting on a vintage linen tablecloth, bathed in soft light that accentuates their fresh curves. In the far right of the photo, a third bok choy looks on jealously.

"That's why we call it 'food porn.' Research shows that sexual imagery sells everything better, from air filters to zucchini."

"Well, I like the old sex just fine. Can't we have both?"

He asks this as I sit down next to him. I scooch slightly over to my side, willing my thigh not to cozy up to his.

"Well, of course." I'm flustered. "The Bee's Knees brand will be all about pleasure, all about flavor and beauty. You can see it here and here."

I tamp down my nervousness by focusing on what I know best. He's nodding, seeing how the site flows. But when I get to the "About" page, he winces.

"Why do you have to have a picture of me?" he says. He's reacting to one of him holding striped beets with a look of amazement and pride. A photo that made Charlotte swoon.

"I've been doing some reading. The food movement is practically a religion now. There are even warring sects, with the locavores and Slow Food folks arguing with the all-organic crowd. We want to focus on the commandments they all agree on, including *Know Thy Farmer*. And you, Sir, are the farmer."

I scroll down to show him the placeholders I set up for the photos I'll take on Friday of the CSA packing team. They're from the *I Love Lucy* episode where Lucille Ball is overwhelmed at the candy factory, her eyes huge under the white cap. I'd hoped for a laugh here, but Roger frowns. Uh-oh.

"We'll show the team, too. Of course I'll want to learn more about your story, how you started the farm and why it's important to you."

"I appreciate all the work you've put into this, but let's stick to selling vegetables. I'm out in the country because I like my privacy. It's bad enough to have to come to the market and answer all those nosy questions."

He hands me back the iPad and stands up. "Most of the site is great, Sophia. Please keep going in that direction. I'll give you a little background on the land when you come out on Friday, but let's keep me and the team off-limits." He puts on his jacket and heads for the door.

"Aye aye, Farmer Branch," I say, following him into the hall. I'm startled by his response. Every candidate demands to be the star. Lame CEO commercials are the lucrative backbone of any local PR industry. How did we go from foot rubs and a tingly elevator ride to this frosty business talk?

Roger sees my concern and reaches out to brush a strand of hair out of my eyes. I come as close as I dare, then lean back against the wall. My breasts rise up toward him, begging to be touched. *So unprofessional!* But this isn't a real job. And right this minute, I'd rather have him kiss me.

He leans forward, then pauses. The light catches his cheekbones again and I see his mind working. In a flash, he reaches a decision — and not one I like. Roger drops his hand and steps away.

"I can see myself out. Come by on Friday at two. Bring your camera and wear those boots."

I sigh as the door closes behind him. I turn on the oven and open the fridge to take out the bowls of dough and apple-raisin filling that Charlotte dropped by yesterday. The idea had been that I'd wow Roger with my baking skills. I also take out a bag of Ghirardelli Semi-Sweet Chocolate Baking Chips. I'll make some of these pockets with the healthy filling Charlotte suggested and some with two tablespoons each of chocolate chips.

I'll ask Jo Lynn up to try them. I bet she'll prefer the version that is hot, sweet, and a little naughty.

Apple-Raisin Pockets

Active time: 30 minutes. Total time: 55 minutes. Serves 6.

Slightly Sweet Dough (page 54)
3 medium Granny Smith apples or other tart apples
3 tablespoons sugar (37 grams)
⅛ teaspoon cinnamon
⅛ teaspoon nutmeg
3 tablespoons water
3 tablespoon raisins

Heat the oven to 400°F with a bread stone on the bottom rack if you have one. Divide Slightly Sweet Dough in half and cover with a clean tea towel while it comes to room temperature.

Cut each apple into quarters and cut out core. Cut each quarter into four long sections, then cut slices across three or four times.

Mix sugar, cinnamon, and nutmeg in a medium pot, add water, and bring to a boil over high heat. Reduce heat to medium low, then add apples. Cook apples uncovered until fork-tender, about 8 minutes. Stir in raisins.

Meanwhile, divide each dough half into 3 pieces (about 120 grams each). Roll out each piece between two pieces of well-floured parchment paper or on a clean, well-floured counter. Heap about ¼ cup apple mixture on bottom half of dough circle and fold dough over apple mixture.

Pinch edges of dough together to seal, then cut three slits in top of each pocket to allow steam to escape while it bakes. Use a table knife to open up slits so they don't seal as the dough rises.

Bake pockets on parchment paper and a bread stone or cookie sheet for 25 to 30 minutes, until lightly browned and juice just starts to bubble out of the slits. Brush off any extra flour and cool for at least 5 minutes.

Serve warm or at room temperature. Best fresh from the oven, but any extra keeps covered at room temperature for about 3 days.

BLUEGRASS NEWGRASS

An old Ford Taurus follows my Prius off the highway and down the one-lane road to Roger's house. Three battered cars covered with bumper stickers are already parked in front of the barn. A redhead gets out of the Taurus, looking like she'd put some bumper stickers on her car, too, if only she hadn't borrowed it from Daddy. Probably "No Farmers, No Food" or "My Other Car is a Tractor."

Roger waves us in from the barn door. It's open wide enough to let a truck pass. Light and fresh air pour in.

"Welcome to CSA Central!" he calls. Red and I follow him in. Roger introduces me to Red, real name Maggie, and three other interns who help him pack the boxes. They are already setting up crates of lettuce, sugar snaps, spring onions, and chard on two long tables. A third table stands between them, an odd contraption like a ladder with rungs made of rolling pins so close together that they nearly touch.

"What's that?"

"You'll see once we get started. Sometimes the best tech is old tech."

Maggie rolls a cart of packing boxes to the far end of the ladder table.

"Ready, girls?" she calls. "Ready!" they reply. Maggie hits a button on the old boom box in the corner. The Judds sing harmony as Maggie grabs the first flat box, squares it up, toggles bottom flaps into place, and sends it rolling down the line. She does a little spin in time to the music and grabs another box to do it again.

On either side of the ladder table, interns take produce from the field crates and place it carefully into the CSA boxes as they roll by. Heavy items like onions and sweet potatoes go in first, then tougher greens, and finally lettuce and a small bundle of asparagus. At the end of the line, Roger checks each box and folds the lid shut, stacking them on wheeled carts that will go back into the walk-in cooler that hums in the rear of the barn.

There's bantering about boyfriends and the sustainable-ag projects at the community college. Roger asks Maggie about her talk on organic farming in drought conditions for the Sustainable Ag conference in the fall. After a few questions and a laugh, she admits she needs to measure the productivity of an industrial farm for comparison.

I listen while taking stills and videos of the women packing. Roger doesn't say much, just tosses in a comment now and then that turns the conversation back to a deeper level. He's practically Socratic, leading them to discover their own wisdom by asking instead of telling.

I focus on getting backlit action shots and close ups with just hands or backs. Might as well honor Roger's weird demand for privacy, even if it's hard to believe anyone here has something to hide.

Fortunately the colorful boxes rolling down the line don't have any such concerns. Maggie puts on a new CD. We all sing along with Carolina Road's happy bluegrass beat:

> *I miss all the simple things from my upbringing.*
> *I'm going back to my roots, where I belong.*

Old-timey agriculture with a modern twist. Ancient ways with modern spice. *I can support this.* Roger grabs me for a quick two-step, then goes to get another cart. When we're done, Roger says, "Why don't you all come in for some of my famous Anasazi bean burgers? I set a batch in the fridge to thaw last night."

Anasazi Bean Burgers

Active time: 25 minutes. Total time: 1 hour. Serves 8.

4 garlic cloves
1 tablespoon finely ground flaxseed (7 grams)
1 tablespoon bean broth or water
1 bunch spring onions (100 grams or 1 cup chopped)

4 cups cooked, well-drained Anasazi, pinto, or black beans (page 23)
1 cup old-fashioned rolled oats (80 grams)
1 tablespoon lemon juice
1 tablespoon cumin
1 teaspoon chipotle
½ teaspoon salt

Drop garlic into a food processor with its cutting blade spinning at top speed and process until garlic quits jumping, about 10 seconds.

Make flaxseed "egg" using just 1 tablespoon bean broth or water and cooking for just 15 seconds (page 36).

Cut spring onions crossways two or three times and pulse in the food processor three or four times until roughly chopped.

Put beans, flaxseed egg, and remaining ingredients in the food processor and process until mixture is well mixed but still a little rough. Let it rest for at least 15 minutes to give oats time to soak up any extra moisture. About 15 minutes before you start to shape the burgers, make sure there's a rack in the center position of your oven and heat the oven to 450°F.

Line a cookie sheet with parchment paper. Divide bean mixture evenly into eight mounds on the parchment paper. Roger uses a vintage lever ice-cream scoop for this because he likes its speed, accuracy, and satisfying *click-plop* sound. Flatten the mounds into burger shapes. Bean burgers don't shrink, so shape them to fit your bun.

Bake for 15 minutes, then use a spatula to turn over. Bake until the other side is browned and crispy but still creamy inside, about 15 minutes. Sometimes the bottom of the burger is more attractive than the top, so don't hesitate to check and flip as needed before serving.

Serve hot on whole-grain buns with your favorite condiments. Cool any extra on wire racks and refrigerate for four days or freeze for up to a year. Reheat thawed bean burgers in a toaster oven or on a grill; they get soft when microwaved.

WATCHING

"One week he's dancing with me in the barn and this week he's too busy to even look at the video," I tell Charlotte.

"Did you step on his feet?"

"No! Everything seemed fine that day. He even knows I was careful not to shoot any footage that would invade his precious privacy."

"As if anyone can have privacy these days!"

"Exactly my point. But he's the boss."

"Well, the close-up action shots really work for this box-packing video. And I love the rhythm you get by cutting back to the pioneer pictures from the History Museum archives. What's the song?"

"That's *Back to My Roots* by Lorraine Jordan and Carolina Road. She taught school in Garner before making it big on the bluegrass charts. She was so nice about giving me permission to use the song, too."

I put on the CD, skipping to my favorite track while Charlotte fetches us two more Bad Penny beers.

"Here's to sad songs and happy days." We clink bottles and listen for awhile. Charlotte and I have long moved beyond the need to chatter every minute.

She stirs after awhile and takes another swig. "Sophia, why all this focus on privacy? Do you think he's married? Or on the lam?"

"Farming is not a great career choice for someone on the run."

"Maybe it is. Especially if what you did before was something completely different."

"Like what?"

"International spy. Rock star. Maybe he's in the witness protection program."

"That's it. No more beers for you. Here, see if you can guess the secret to my new baked-beans recipe. I might be starting to get the hang of this slow cooker."

Un-Baked Beans

Active time: 10 minutes. Total time: at least 40 minutes, ideally at least twelve hours. Makes 10 servings.

1 pound dried pinto beans (4½ cups cooked) (454 grams)
1 yellow onion
½ cup unsulphured molasses
2 tablespoons prepared bold or yellow mustard
1 tablespoon smooth peanut butter
1 tablespoon tahini
¼ cup tomato paste

Active time: 10 minutes. Total time: at least 40 minutes, ideally at least twelve hours. Makes 10 servings.

Cook pinto beans in slow cooker with only five cups water (page 23), adding more water only as needed to keep beans barely covered.

When beans are nearly tender, chop onion and stir into beans with molasses, peanut butter, and tahini. Continue cooking covered on high until beans and onions are tender, about 30 minutes. Stir in tomato paste.

Serve immediately or, better yet, pour into another container to speed cooling, let cool for up to two hours, and then refrigerate overnight so the sauce flavors work their way through the pintos. Serve hot over rice, baked potatoes, or as a side dish. Good for breakfast with toast, too, British B&B style. Keep any extra refrigerated for up to four days or frozen for up to a year.

❈

HOP-A-LONG HEART

Ding! The elevator doors open, releasing three men in sharp gray suits. Guys with jobs, and good ones, from the looks of their tailoring. They step past me into the lobby. I moan to myself when I spot Jo Lynn's holiday-du-jour outfit: a vest with pastel Easter eggs. The color progression is elegant and the stitching refined, even if it does seem to say *celebrate or experience the consequences.*

Does that woman live in the elevator? I'm not in the mood for chipper. Except for a terse email approving the video, Roger has barely talked to me since the day we packed boxes.

"Chocolate?" Jo Lynn asks, looking up from the cellophane bag she's torn open. "I'm making Easter baskets for my nephews." She holds out a nugget wrapped in a red foil the same vibrant intensity as her deep pink nails. In fact, her offering is a whole holiday behind her outfit and Easter-basket plans. "This Valentine's candy was buy one, get one. The boys are too young to tell bunnies from hearts."

"Don't you always get one when you buy one?"

She looks at me like I'm an idiot. The elevator doors close.

"OK, buy one get one *free*, Miss Sourpuss. I bet you don't even clip."

"Clip?"

"Coupons. I saved $22.15 today. And I'm putting $20 right in the pool."

I can't help myself. "Pool?"

"Girl, the basketball pool! Who's going to win the NCAA! How can you not know about that when everybody here lives and breathes basketball?"

She gets out at her floor. Was it neighborliness or just pity that made her turn and say, "Ask Roger. He runs the durn thing."

Roger? Sports? My teeth crack through the hollow heart. Maybe I wasn't any more observant than Jo Lynn's nephews.

Countdown Trail Mix

Active time: 3 minutes. Total time: 3 minutes. Makes 20 servings, ⅓ cup each.

400 grams peanuts, such as Whole Foods Market's 365 brand lightly salted organic peanuts)
300 grams Ghirardelli semi-sweet chocolate chips
200 grams raisins
100 grams walnut pieces

Combine all ingredients in a jar or bowl, breaking walnut pieces up into peanut-sized pieces with a knife or your fingers if desired. Mix well.

Store in a jar topped with a measuring cup to encourage moderate portion sizes. A one-third-cup size works if you can bring yourself to serve it level. Use a one-quarter cup measure if you prefer "heaping" servings.

THE DEEP END

Maybe everyone else went crazy about basketball, but my family's favorite sport was always politics. Why root for something that didn't really matter? Wasn't it more fun to canvas and maybe really help your team instead of counting on your lucky socks or how loud you yelled at the TV to make a difference?

I google "basketball North Carolina" and get over a hundred million hits. OK, maybe Jo Lynn is right about the importance of the big orange ball.

I watch some clips on YouTube and read up on the local teams. The Triangle turns out to be the epicenter of the Atlantic Coast Conference, with Duke, Carolina, and NC State all within twenty-five miles of each other.

I find myself enjoying the highlight reels. Such strength and grace! So much faster than football, and with more revealing uniforms.

The controversies when the refs and coaches argue about subterfuge on the court are the best. Had they witnessed a violation, a personal foul, or a flagrant foul? Evidently arguing too hard with the refs was yet another kind of no-no: *T* for technical foul.

I watch one clip five times until I can see the screen, the block, the assist, the fake, and — yes! — the shot for three points.

I look at the schedule again and realize that Roger began avoiding me just when the big games of the season started. Thinking back, I remember that the Senator's campaign never scheduled big events on Wednesday (church night) or on game days.

This week was the Sweet Sixteen regional competition and next week the Final Four. By then, he might forget me all together. Time to hatch a plan.

I gather intel in the Park & Market gym and at the bagel place. I make a few reconnaissance runs and map out my campaign strategy.

I pick up my CSA box on Saturday, lingering by the Starbucks until Roger is alone. I walk up, put the box on his table, and slap a $20 bill on top.

"I want in."

He hisses, "Put that away. What are you trying to do?"

"If you can take Jo Lynn's money, why not mine. I want in on the basketball pool."

"Keep your voice down. Gambling, even a basketball pool, is technically against the law. Don't get me in trouble with Mr. Henry."

I shove the money in my coat pocket.

"Well, you do it anyway, don't you?"

"Who wants to know?"

"I do. A novice fan. I've gotten a taste of this thing called basketball and find it quite exciting."

I lean over the table and give him my best *oh officer!* look, chin down and looking up through my eyelashes. "Please teach me about basketball. I'll take you to the biggest screen around and ply you with microbrews and the best black-bean burger this side of Santa Fe."

"Avocado?"

"And sweet-potato fries."

"Game on."

Sweet Sixteen Oatmeal Raisin Bars

Active time: 16 minutes. Total time: 46 minutes. Serves 16.

½ cup apple sauce (128 grams)
2 flaxseed "eggs" (page 36)
2 cups old-fashioned rolled oats (190 grams)
1 cup white whole wheat flour (120 grams)
¾ cup brown sugar (165 grams)
1 teaspoon baking soda
1¼ teaspoons cinnamon
½ teaspoon nutmeg
¼ teaspoon salt
1 teaspoon vanilla
1 cup walnut pieces (110 grams), coarsely chopped
1 cup raisins (160 grams)
oil or shortening for the pan

Heat oven to 350°F. Grease a 13 x 9-inch baking pan.

Stir apple sauce and flaxseed eggs until well combined and let come to room temperature. Put oats, flour, brown sugar, baking soda, cinnamon, nutmeg, and salt into a mixing bowl. Mix on low speed using an electric mixer until well combined, about 30 seconds. Add apple-sauce mixture and vanilla and mix on low until well combined and evenly moist. Stir in walnuts and raisins.

Spread dough evenly in prepared baking pan and bake for 25 to 30 minutes, until top just begins to turn golden brown. Let cool in the pan set on a wire rack, then cut into 16 bars. Keeps covered at room temperature for about four days and freezes well.

BELLE OF THE BALLS

Y ou do know that basketball is different than bowling," Roger
says, stopping dead in front of Sparians.

"Trust me," I say, grabbing Roger's arm and steering him through the door of the bowling alley. We both blink as our eyes adjust to the dimly lit interior. A traditional bar is on the right. Clusters of cozy pleather couches are on the left, each group facing a bowling lane.

At the end of each lane is an enormous screen, each showing an announcer talking earnestly, with basketball players taking practice shots in the background.

"Bowling and basketball, sir" I say, sweeping my arm aside in a gesture of welcome. "We have lane six all to ourselves."

"But you can't hear the announcers!"

"No worries. I brought a headphone splitter and two sets of earplugs so we can listen to the announcer on my phone. And we can bowl during the commercials and at half time."

"Or I can school you in the noble art of basketball."

"Even better."

We walk down to the last lane. Sparians is set up for casual bowling, with bumpers instead of gutters so the ball always goes down the lane. We settle in side-by-side on the couch, so we can both look straight at our big screen. Roger's eyes widen with delight when the waitress brings us our bean burgers, sweet potato fries, and a pair of cold Big Boss ales. We clink bottles and trade sips: my pale Helle's Belle for his dark Night Knight.

I lean close so I can hear him describe a sport he clearly loves. He puts his arm around my shoulder and pulls me closer for a few minutes. But once the teams start scoring in earnest, he leans forward and pounds both fists on his knees.

"Pass it, pass it, kick it out to the wing... yes! Three from downtown!"

I lean forward with him so the earplugs aren't ripped from my ear. By the end of the first half, our thighs are pressed together, knee to hip.

As the game progresses, I learn why he loves this sport above all others. He teaches me to look for the set plays, where three or even four players might handle the ball before a shot is made. I see how much nerve is needed to shoot a free throw, especially after someone has just knocked you clear under the basket and your team is down by only two points.

When a hail-Mary shot goes in just before the final buzzer, Roger whoops and leaps up, pulling me up with him. He embraces me with the rough hug of victory that one fan might give another.

But instead of releasing me, Roger shifts, holding our embrace a beat longer than should really be done amidst children's birthday parties. I wrap my arms around his waist and press my cheek against his chest. He smells of sweet potatoes and fresh air, with an undercurrent of healthy man.

After a moment, I pull back and look up at him. "How about a post-game interview in my locker room upstairs?"

"Does it have a shower?"

"Oh yes. Big enough for a little one-on-one."

It's a good thing the elevator was empty when we got on. If a ref had been there, surely he would have called us for a flagrant holding violation.

Sweet-Potato Oven Fries

Active time: 5 minutes. Total time: 45 minutes. Serves 4.

1 pound sweet potatoes
2 teaspoons olive oil
coarse-grained salt to taste

Heat oven to 450°F, with a rack in the center position. For easy cleanup, line a rimmed cookie sheet with parchment paper.

Scrub but do not peel sweet potatoes. Cut them into quarters to create flat sides so you can safely cut them, then cut into oven-fry shapes about ½ inch across and about 3 inches long. Toss with olive oil, arrange into a single layer, and sprinkle with salt. Use another cookie sheet if needed, but don's stack the fries.

These fries brown first on the bottom. If you have the energy, carefully and quickly turn potatoes over using a thin spatula after about 20 minutes of roasting so they brown on both sides. Bake until well browned but not burned for 35 to 40 minutes total.

Serve hot with ketchup if desired.

ENJOYING THE JOURNEY

My urgent need to jump Roger's bones makes my hands shake so badly I can barely get my apartment key in the lock. Once inside, I turn my face up to Farmer Bee, hoping for a kiss before we got down and dirty. Yes! Without breaking lip-lock, I pull at his flannel shirt, searching for his buttons. One pops off and pings against my door.

Roger pulls back and fingers a dangling thread.

"Wait a minute," he says. He takes my face between his hands and gazed into my eyes. "There's only one first time, Sophia. Let's slow down and do it right."

Slow down! I want him now, as feverishly as the crowds at the basketball playoffs wanted their teams to win.

But I'm not with a sweaty college kid, fumbling for a basketball or a bra hook. I'm not with goal-oriented Kenny, who gave me the choice of hurrying along or longing for more.

Roger moves like a man who thinks in terms of seasons. A man who enjoys the process more than he enjoys ticking a task off his to-do list.

I hold Roger close to me, stroking his strong back through his shirt, then under it. He lifts me up onto the granite counter, looks at me, then turns on my reading light next to the love seat.

"Sophia, you are so beautiful. Such skin! Such amazing curves."

I make a face, suddenly thinking of how exposed I am up here. He comes close again and runs his thumb along my jaw.

"You're a goddess. Don't ever doubt that. Look what you've done to me!"

I look, then words are over. My thoughts of the past and future vanish. Only now. Only this man. His breath becomes my breath, his desire mine. I call what I can of his name.

"Bee!"

Bliss.

We move to my bedroom, where we explore each other's pleasure until we're exhausted. We wake at dawn for coffee and breakfast cake, then start again.

If this were a game, we'd be well into overtime, even on to the next round in the tournament. But we're not scratching a private itch or competing with each other. We're more playful and serious than that. We're coupling. Taking a leap into love.

Chocolate Sweet-Potato Breakfast Cake

Active time: 15 minutes. Total time: about an hour. Makes 8
servings.

2 flaxseed eggs (page 36)
1 cup white whole wheat flour (120 grams)
⅓ cup cocoa (30 grams)
½ teaspoon salt
½ teaspoon baking soda
½ cup coconut oil, room temperature
shortening for pan or eight paper cupcake liners
1 cup sugar (200 grams)
²/₃ cup mashed sweet potatoes (140 grams)

Preheat oven to 350°F. Make flaxseed eggs and let cool to room
temperature.

Whisk dry ingredients in a small bowl to blend. Put coconut
oil and sugar in a mixing bowl and cream together on medium
speed for about 1 minute. Grease an 8 x 8-inch pan or put 8 paper
liners in a muffin tin. Add flaxseed eggs to sugar mixture and beat
on medium speed for about a minute. Mix in sweet potato and then
mix in dry ingredients.

Spread batter in pan. Bake for 45 to 50 minutes (30 minutes for
cupcakes), until a tester inserted into cake's center comes out clean.

Let cool for at least 10 minutes. Store any extra covered at room
temperature or wrap well and freeze. Enjoy as a snack cake after
school or as part of a naughty breakfast.

CHICKEN CARAVAN

For the first time in my life, I can look forward to sporting events. My favorite part is still half-time. It's not for the cheer leaders or the musical acts anymore, though. Now it's for the way Roger warms me up for the post-game fireworks.

It's like I suddenly have infrared vision, too. I understand things that have been around me all the time. At the market, the odd outfits make sense when I recognize team colors or mascots. Thinking back, I can even understand why the Senator used to tell us we needed to get out of the paint or to watch the shot clock.

On the Sunday between the Final Four and the championship game, I drive out to Roger's to see what he's described as the changing of the fields. I wear my boots and a wind breaker, but pack a small bag with a tooth brush and something lacy just in case.

June, Patsy, and Dolly dash about, encouraging Roger and me to walk faster up the hill to the north fields. As we come over the crest of the hill, I see three big pigs in the field to the west. To the east, a dozen chickens peck around what looks like a gypsy trailer.

"Are you running a campground now, Farmer Bee?"

"Just housing for the Golden Girls. I got tired of picking Japanese beetles off the corn and beans. I met some folks on the Tour d' Coup that wanted a good home for chickens who'd aged past their laying years. These old hens don't lay eggs, but they do eat their weight in pests. They keep the weeds down too."

"What about the pigs?"

"Fads gone bad. People went crazy over pot-bellied pigs a while ago, then started abandoning them when they realized they grew up and needed to eat and get exercise every day."

"Come on, Hildi! Come on Gullin and Circe!" Roger calls to the pigs, taking a handful of gnarly carrots from his pocket. They trot over, looking like collie-sized hippos with rough black hair.

"They're not as pot-bellied as the ones I've seen on TV."

"No, these girls get exercise and plenty of veggies. These carrots are too ugly for the CSA boxes, but the pigs like them fine" he says, walking toward a gate that separates the pig pasture from the collard field. Hildi and Gullin follow him eagerly. Patsy herds Circe so she goes along too.

A golden barn cat watches from on top of a fence post, staying clear of the dogs.

"Sylvester loves the pigs, but the dogs make her nervous. She'll go back with them once we start moving the chickens."

He closes the gate behind the pigs, who have finished the carrots and started rooting around the collard stumps.

"They're like little composting machines," Roger tells me. "They polish off the remains of each crop. Then we wheel in the chicken wagon, so the chickens will break up what the pigs leave behind, digging for grubs. Fewer flies and beetles plus another layer of manure. In a few weeks, we'll move them again and I'll plant peppers here."

"All that manure and I mostly smell clover."

"As Joel Salatin says, 'Good food production should be aesthetically and aromatically, sensually romantic.' That's true for our farm-working animals too. If you don't keep them crammed into sheds or feed lots, they don't smell any worse than a few wet dogs."

We grab the wagon tongue and pull the chicken wagon to the field that the pigs just left. Some chickens follow and the rest continue to peck where they were.

"We'll leave the gate between these two pastures open until tomorrow. By sundown, the chickens will come over here to roost, safe from the owls and other varmints."

Turns out it's a good thing I packed a bag. I don't return to my home pasture until after the big game on Monday night. Early Tuesday morning, Roger shows me how to make a scramble using wild chickweed and chives. Two big handfuls of the tender, white-bloomed plant cook down to a few mouthfuls in minutes, perfect for a fast breakfast.

"Chickpea flour is funny," he says. "I get it at one of the Indian groceries on Chatham Street in Cary. They call it besan flour. Bob's Red Mill sells bags of it as 'garbanzo-bean flour' at Whole Foods."

When we get done eating, I decide to track some of the flour down for myself, no matter what name it goes by.

Chickweed Chickpea Scramble

Active time: 10 minutes. Total time: 15 minutes. Serves 2.
½ cup chickpea flour (60 grams)
½ teaspoon salt
few grinds of pepper
¾ cup water
1 cups chickweed or arugula
2 tablespooons chopped chives
1¼ teaspoons canola oil, divided

Stir chickpea flour, salt, and pepper in a medium bowl. Add half the water and stir until smooth. Add remaining water and stir again. (Make-ahead tip: do this the night before and refrigerate.)

Rinse chickweed and chop coarsely into two-inch chunks. Snip chives into one-inch pieces.

Heat ¼ teaspoon canola oil in a medium well-seasoned cast-iron skillet or a nonstick skillet over medium heat. Cook chickweed and chives until wilted, about 3 minutes, stirring occasionally. Give batter another stir and pour over chickweed. Use a spatula to scrape scramble from bottom of pan as it cooks and to stir the mixture as you would scrambled eggs. The batter will tend to stick, but that makes crispy parts for the scramble. When scramble comes together in a heap after about 5 minutes, put it on a cutting board for about 5 minutes so bean flour absorbs liquid and becomes more digestible.

Using the spatula or a knife, break up scramble into chucks that would take two or three bites to eat.

Warm scramble by heating remaining oil in the skillet over medium heat, adding scramble, and cooking it for about 2 minutes. Serve hot.

STOCKING UP

"Triple Coupon Day at the Teeter!" Jo Lynn says as she wedges a grocery cart further into the elevator.

"Are you getting ready for the zombie apocalypse? Auditioning for *Hoarders*?" I ask. Her cart is full to the top, with a dozen big cans of tomatoes, six jars of peanut butter, and boxes of tea bags. A chocolate bunny rides on a small mountain of brown sugar and cocoa powder next to a three-ring binder labeled *Clip or Be Clipped*.

"Laugh if you want, but this is how I afford organic tomatoes and my subscription to Roger's CSA. It's simple economics. Buy low, eat high."

"Yes, but why so much?"

"Why not? I got a 37% return on my grocery budget last year, just by watching sales and stashing canned goods under my bed. It's a safer investment than the stock market."

I look at her with new appreciation. An organized person with a firm grasp of home economics was just who I needed to fight off my own apocalypse.

"Jo Lynn, can you help me? I've got a refrigerator full of greens and just can't keep up. Would you show me what you do? Please?"

"Happy to," Jo Lynn says. Her hand reaches out to stroke the binder with pride. "Let me put this stuff away and I'll be up in a flash. I want you to try the cookies I baked last night too."

As she rolls her grocery cart down the hall, the bunny on the back of her holiday sweater bids me to "have a hoppy, hoppy Easter."

Bunny Luv Cocoa Cookies

Active time: 20 minutes. Total time: 30 minutes. Makes 12
servings, 3 cookies each. Doubles well.

1 flaxseed "egg" (page 36)
14 tablespoons sugar (¾ cup plus two tablespoons) (175
grams)
6 tablespoons Earth Balance Natural Buttery Spread, at room
temperature (85 grams or 3 ounces)
1 cup white whole wheat flour (120 grams)
6 tablespoons Ghirardelli Natural Unsweetened Cocoa (36
grams)
½ teaspoon baking soda
scant ¼ teaspoon salt
2 tablespoons sorghum or honey
1 teaspoon vanilla

Heat oven to 350°F. Make flaxseed egg and let cool to
room temperature. Beat sugar and buttery spread with an electric mixer until fluffy, about 2 minutes on medium. Whisk
remaining dry ingredients together in a medium bowl, then add
to sugar mixture with flaxseed egg, sorghum, and vanilla. Stir
until just well combined. (Over stirring means tough cookies.)

Drop cookie dough onto an ungreased cookie sheet. (Jo
Lynn lines her cookie sheets with parchment paper to make
cleanup easier.)

Bake for 8 to 10 minutes, then allow to cool for 2 minutes
until firm enough to lift with a spatula onto a cooling rack or
clean brown-paper bag. Eat a few warm, then thoroughly cool
the rest and store in a cookie jar or other container on your
counter.

ENDLESS WAVES OF GREEN

"Ooo-whee, girl, you are going to be in trouble if Roger sees this!" Jo Lynn declares. I nod. Before I met Roger, my fridge had been a pristine cave of cold, the white and glass vista broken only by a few oranges, my collection of hot sauce, and diet sodas. Now bags of greens fill every shelf. Some are still fresh, but others are long past their prime. I feel like I am snorkeling over a big bed of kelp. The hot-pink pickles and golden jar of salad dressing gleam from the door shelves like tropical fish.

"Let's turn this puppy off and start by sorting." I tap the off switch and Jo Lynn started pulling out bags.

"Let's line them up here, from prima-donna asparagus to workhorses like collards and cabbage. At least you've got them wrapped right."

"Charlotte showed me how. And I cut the leaves from the roots. But now I've got bags and bags of carrot and beet leaves. She has all those big dinner parties so she uses everything up and more every week. But I'm not about to inflict my cooking on my friends."

She picks up a bag of wilted lettuce. "Don't be so hard on yourself. We got to this just in time. You can cook lettuce too. It shrinks right down so one person can eat a whole head at a sitting." She sets it by the sink to be cleaned and pulls open the bottom drawer. "As for these roots, let's start with the turnips since they go bad first. I see you've got pickles going, but my mama always cooked them with their greens."

"Just don't throw anything out! Roger will kill me."

Jo Lynn smiles. and reaches into her canvas bag. She pulls out a big glass jar with a wide mouth.

"Killing ain't got nothing to do with what Roger wants to do to you. Take a deep breath and I'll show you how to make my Daddy's favorite sandwich. Then we'll put this jar to work."

Hot-Collards Courage Sandwich

Active time: 10 minutes. Total time: 10 minutes. Yield: 1 sandwich. Making more sandwiches takes about an extra 2 minutes total apiece.

1½ cup chopped collards, about two medium leaves
¼ cup sliced yellow or sweet onion
¼ teaspoon olive oil
⅛ teaspoon ground chipotle or cayenne powder
2 slices Good Whisk Bread from *Wildly Affordable Organic* or other whole-grain bread
2 tablespoons peanut butter
scattering Hot-Pink Refrigerator Pickles (page 40), especially pickled beets
salt to taste

Cut or pull stems away from collard leaves. Chop stems into quarter-inch pieces. Cut leaves into strips about ¼ inch by 3 inches. Quarter and slice onion.

Pour olive oil in a large pot and spread with your fingers to cover the bottom, then heat on medium low. Add chipotle, stir, then add collard stems and onion. Cook for about 4 minutes, until onion starts to soften. Add collard leaves, cover, and turn heat down to low. Steam until collard leaves are chewy-tender, about 4 minutes.

Toast bread, then spread with peanut butter on both slices. Heap one slice with well-drained, cooked collards, top with pickles, and then top with other slice of bread.

Jo Lynn's daddy liked his sandwich cut in half diagonally. He'd eat it hot while imagining glorious outcomes and dreams come true.

SHE STOUPS TO CONQUER

Even after the surprisingly tasty sandwich, I'm overwhelmed by the piles of greens from the piles of produce on my counter. I blink and scan. Asparagus, lettuce, Swiss chard, beet greens, mustard greens, bok choy, carrot tops, two kinds of kale, and collards, sorted by tenderness and stage of decay.

"Now let's get stoup-ed!" Jo Lynn shakes the jar she'd set on my counter. "We'll start you in the habit of making stew-soup. It's the secret to not wasting anything. Plus you get a free lunch every few weeks. We'll cook a mess of this stuff today after we have our smoothies. But from now on, keep this jar in your freezer. Add your scraps: half an onion, a few bites of carrots, the beans you didn't finish. When it fills up, thaw it out and cook it up. Free lunch!"

"Sounds like the minestrone my Zia Donatella used to make."

"You got it. Add some noodles if you have them. I even add anything from a take-out box that I haven't eaten by the next day. Some things make it nasty: mayonnaise, marshmallows, hot dogs." She gives a little shudder, making her Easter-egg earrings tinkle. "But if you just keep your Aunt's minestrone in mind, you'll be fine."

"Why do you think Roger makes such a big deal about not wasting anything?"

"Oh child, he knows how hard it is to grow! And he knows that every tiny bit could be used to feed somebody or come back to feed the fields. But so many folks send it right into the landfill or down the drain and out to sea. It's enough to break a farmer's heart."

"Feed the fields? Like those peas Roger grows that make the soil better?"

"Right. It wasn't too long ago that we saved everything. My granddad fed what he couldn't eat to his chickens and pigs. Then he'd used their poop to feed the fields, if you'll pardon my French. The new old-fashioned farms like Roger's are trying to do that again, only even smarter."

"So he wants to save money on fertilizer."

"It's more than that. He's working with the cycle of life, death, and rebirth. Soil fed like this is alive, full of little critters and micro-somethings that make the food better for you and better able to make it thorough hot dry spells. 'Roger even says it's important for national security."

I laugh. "Poop against pirates?"

"More like poop against politics. Factory farms throw away the poop of the poor animals they cage up. So much of it washes down the Mississippi that created a big dead zone in the Gulf. They basically just use the soil as a way to hold their plants in place while they douse them with fertilizers and poisons made from oil. That washes downstream too. Lots of the oil comes from the Middle East. I shouldn't have to tell you how that means politics."

"I hadn't thought of it that way! And the oil that doesn't come from there we're trying to get out of Alaska or from Canadian tar sands, as dirty as source as you can get. There was that big march on Washington just last week about that."

"Now you're catching on. Makes you wonder how many of those folks who marched bother to have a Stoup jar in their freezer."

Stoup

Add scraps of anything that might make a good vegetables soup to a jar in your freezer. When it's full or you want a free lunch, thaw the jar overnight in the fridge.

The next day, dump the jar into a pot and bring to a boil. Add anything that needs to be used up: wilting carrots, soft potatoes, left-over pasta sauce, and greens, greens, greens. Reduce heat and simmer until vegetables are soft. Taste and add lemon juice, hot sauce, or canned diced tomatoes to brighten the flavor if needed. Serve hot. Refrigerate any extra.

BIRTHDAY

Roger pushes back his plate with a big smile and folds his hands on his belly.

"Aren't you the little lady who told me you don't know how to cook?"

I nod and blush, relieved and proud that lunch had gone so well. Having him here was my secret birthday present to myself.

Charlotte came over last night to help me make the cake for strawberry shortcake. This morning, I'd gotten three pints of perfectly ripe berries from Roger at the market. Rather than staying around to help with the booth, I'd come back here to slice half the berries and whirl the other half in the blender with a little sugar. As Charlotte promised, mixing the sliced berries with the blended ones created a perfect sauce for the shortcake.

Roger stands up and stretches, giving me a chance to see how his back muscles fan out. He isn't handsome in a movie-star way. Instead, his magnetism comes from raw vitality and fitness. Having him look so downright yummy at fifty one made me feel not so bad about turning forty five. In fact, I feel better now than I have in years.

Suddenly, I feel worse. Roger is heading for the door, just minutes after he'd finished eating! I'd hoped for a little second dessert over in the love seat.

"Farmer Bee, do you really have to buzz out of here so soon?"

"No, not at all. I'm just getting a little something out of my jacket." He returns with a small box, wrapped in batik-printed paper and topped with a blue and purple ribbon.

My jaw drops. "What's that?!?"

"Just a little something for your birthday. I asked Charlotte when it was the week after you first came out to the farm. I thought it might be good for us to have an excuse to celebrate. As if we need an excuse."

He walked over to kiss me, lips still sweet from the strawberries. He took my hand and led me over to the loveseat.

"Sit down and open this up. It's not much, but I hope you'll like it."

I tried to be lady-like, but wind up tearing open the package like an eight-year-old at Christmas. Inside the small box rests an elegant carving of a horse at full gallop, mane flying in the breeze. I gasp and lift it carefully from its cotton bedding. The wood is a deep golden brown, with a pattern I don't recognize. The carving works with the wood's burl pattern to make the horse look so alive I almost expect to hear his hooves pound on the coffee table.

"Roger, I don't know what to say! It's…. He's gorgeous! Did Charlotte tell you about my fetish for horse statues?"

"No, I saw that myself the first time I came up here. And you talk about horses a lot too. I carved this statue from a section of old chestnut beam we found when we redid the kitchen at the farm."

"*You* carved this?"

"Got a little art training from back in the old days. Carving helps pass the dark winter nights."

I kneel before him and lean in until his knees press against my sides and my hands are behind his back. His arms go around me, pulling me close.

"Thank you so much! This is the best present in … in I don't know how long. Nobody has made something this beautiful just for me before."

I get up and rearrange my other lucky horses to give Chestnut the place of honor on the window ledge. If I didn't nag Kenny, he forgot my birthday. When he did remember, he took me to his favorite restaurant and gave me some uncomfortable lingerie. Kenny's idea of a good present to me was for him to get lucky after a big steak dinner.

This year, I am the one who feels lucky. I want to show my new man some serious gratitude.

"Farmer Bee, come here and see how perfect my new stallion looks."

He looks over my shoulder, giving me a chance to lean back into his warmth. He cups my breasts. I wiggle back and feel him stiffen.

Rug burn isn't so bad if you get it for the right reasons.

Coconut Cake with Strawberries

Active time: 20 minutes. Total time: 50 minutes. Serves 12.
2 flaxseed "eggs" (page 36)

½ cup coconut milk (homemade or So Delicious unsweetened organic coconut milk beverage)
1 tablespoon coconut spread (14 grams)
1½ cup sugar, divided (300 grams)
1 cup white whole wheat flour (120 grams)
1⅛ teaspoon baking powder
shortening or oil for the pan
2 pounds strawberries (900 grams)

Heat oven to 375°F. Grease and flour an 8 x 8-inch pan. Heat coconut milk and coconut spread in a microwave-safe container on high for about 90 seconds, until milk begins to steam.

Put 1 cup sugar, flour, and baking powder in a mixing bowl and mix with an electric mixer on low for about thirty seconds, until well combined. Add flaxseed eggs and hot coconut milk. Using an electric mixer, beat on low to until dry ingredients are dampened, about 15 seconds, then on high for 45 seconds. Pour batter into pan and bake immediately for 30 minutes.

Hull strawberries. Slice half into a bowl. Put remaining berries and sugar into a blender and whir on high until nearly smooth, about 20 seconds. Pour strawberry sauce over sliced berries, cover, and refrigerate.

Cake is done when the top is firm and a tester comes out clean. It will not be very tall. Let cake cool completely in the pan on a wire rack.

To serve, cut cake into squares and slice in half horizontally. Spoon strawberry sauce over the bottom half, top with rest of cake, and spoon on more strawberry sauce. Because you're not wasting calories on whipped cream, you can have extra fruit.

DRESSING THE PART

I feel excited, a little nervous even, as I drive to the farm. Roger had asked me if I wanted to play his favorite game today, but wouldn't tell me what it was. He'd just said to wear clean clothes but no fragrance, not even perfume or deodorant.

Badminton was my old childhood favorite, but I couldn't imagine Roger playing anything less physical than full-out tennis. *As long as it's outside!*

A cluster of late-flowering dogwoods gleam at the edge of the dark pine forest as I park near the farmhouse. Roger is arranging something in the back of his red pickup truck. He's wearing wheat-colored jeans and a pale denim shirt with a natural authority that the Calvin Klein models just dream of. Spring sings through my body. *Maybe indoor games wouldn't be so bad after all.*

Roger lifts up something big and white, gives it a shake, and puts it on his head. When he turns to face me, he looks like an astronaut with a hand-made space helmet. A net obscures his face so I can't read his expression. He pulls on thick white gloves.

"Danger, Will Robinson!" I say in my best robot voice, holding my elbows tight to my waist and swinging my hands in circles.

"No danger if you do it right," he says. "Are your clothes clean?"

"Yes, and they always are. Do you think I come here straight from my hot-yoga class? And what sort of game do you have in mind. Dress-up?"

"Not dress-up, protection. Hop in the truck and let's go harvest some honey." He puts what I now recognize as a beekeepers' hat back into the truck.

We drive up a one-lane dirt road into the woods near the river. As we bump along, Roger tells me to put my cell-phone on vibrate and to not make any sudden movements or noise when we're near the hives.

"What if I get stung?"

"You'll be pretty far away from the bees and I've got an extra beekeeper's getup for you. You should be fine."

"But what if …"

"Sophia, I wouldn't put you in danger. Just don't get any closer than you feel comfortable doing. Stinging is a bee's last defense; he dies if he stings you. But just in case they get spooked or you're allergic, I've got ice packs and an Epi-pen right here."

The forest changes from pine and dogwood to bigger hardwoods. In a clearing, six bee hives stand on wooden benches. Bees fly in and out of the hives. A low hum like purring surf fills the air.

The trees that ring the clearing have millions of pale yellow flowers. I pick one up from the ground. It looks tropical, with pointy petals and an orange center.

"Tulip poplars," says Roger. "Their nectar makes my favorite kind of honey. Some folks swear by sourwood honey from the mountains, but this is more mellow."

He shows me how to put on the beekeeper's venilated jumpsuit, netted hat, and gloves. "Don't be nervous. Bees want nectar, not blood. Just don't make any sudden moves and stay back here by this sapling. Breathe."

I look through the netting into his green eyes and breath in deeply through my nose, hold it, hold it, and exhale through my mouth. I nod. He winks and suits up himself.

Roger lights a little pot that turns out to be a smoker, then puffs calming smoke into the hive nearest me. I imagine the bees becoming docile and eating honey inside the hive, as Roger had told me they would.

He lifts off the lid and pulls out a frame. Using a big sharp knife and four quick cuts, he slices off most of the honey-soaked comb and drops it into a bucket. The inch of comb left across the top will give them a starting point for rebuilding it. He replaces the frame and repeats the process until the bucket is half full.

He moves with sure graceful speed. Once his arm jerks as he gets stung, but he doesn't make a sound.

Five minutes later, he walks back toward me. The honeycomb has warped to fit into the bucket. Sunlight makes the honey glow golden and intensifies its sweet fragrance. I breath deeply again, silently thanking the bees for pollinating the crops and for making honey.

"Let's get these suits off and get this back to the house. We'll use a centrifuge to spin off the honey. I trade the beeswax with Eve for candles."

Thank you, bees, for the beeswax too.

Core Recipe: Cashew Cream

Active time: 2 minutes. Total time: 23 minutes. Makes 1 cup.

1 cup organic raw cashews (112 grams)
¾ cup plus 2 tablespoons water

Put cashews and water into a food processor fitted with the cutting blade or into a blender. Process for about 30 seconds. Let rest while cashews soften, about 20 minutes. (Make-ahead tip: soak cashews for several hours or overnight and skip the initial whir and wait.)

Process cashews for about a minute on high until smooth, scraping down the sides if needed. Chill to thicken if desired. Serve over fruit or use as a garnish instead of sour cream or yogurt. Refrigerate any extra for up to four days.

Strawberry Cashew Soup

Active time: 5 minutes. Total time: 5 minutes, possibly more for chilling. Serves 4.

⅓ cup cashew cream (see above) (106 grams)
1 pound strawberries (454 grams)
1½ teaspoons honey (10 grams)
pinch salt

Put soup bowls in the refrigerator to chill. Hull strawberries. Slice four pretty strawberries and set aside for garnish.

Process cashew cream, remaining strawberries, honey, and salt in a food processor fitted with the cutting blade or in a blender until smooth. Taste and add more honey if needed. Cihll soup for 30 minutes if you didn't start with cold strawberries and cashew cream.

Ladle soup carefully into chilled bowls and gently float strawberry slices on top. Refrigerate any extra for up to 4 days.

BIRDS, NOT BUSES

Tweets and love calls work their way into my dream, waking me up. Dawn turns the white cotton curtains of Roger's bedroom rosy pink. No traffic, just the sounds of summer on the farm.

I wriggle against him as we spoon under the sheet. His right hand cups my left breast, thumb twitching in sleep just over my heart. I feet his early morning hardness through the t-shirt he'd lent me to wear to bed. So close. I didn't need lace to feel this bliss.

I sigh. *What was that smell?* I inhale deeply, getting a whiff of Happy Couple plus something else. Bread baking! How? Who?

I slip out of his embrace and stumble sleepily into the kitchen, drawn by elemental fragrance. Home. Hearth. Family.

Something new stands on the blue tile next to the coffee pot. A vintage Dak bread machine! The round top and squat body makes it look like R2D2.

The machine clicks, then starts up a small fan to cool the bread. I peer through the glass dome. Sure enough, it baked a perfect loaf of bread while we slept.

"Where did you go, Sorghum?" Roger wraps his arms around my waist and kisses the top of my head.

"Your baker woke me up. I never figured you for a bread-machine guy."

"Please. He's a house robot. I call him Norbert. He got me out of bed many a morning back when I had an inside job. Something about that smell. I set him up last night while you checked your email."

The coffee pot starts to hiss and spit. Six o'clock.

"Does your coffee machine have a name too?"

Roger looks sheepish. "All the house bots have names. That's Cherry 2000. Why don't you pour us a couple of cups while I slice the bread? I traded some tomatoes last week for a jar of Eden Farm's fig-and-ginger jam."

Good Bread-Machine Bread, Whisk Style

Active time: 5 minutes. Total time: 3 hours. Makes one loaf with about 16 half-moon slices.

2¼ teaspoons rapid-rise or instant yeast (one packet)
2 cups unbleached all-purpose flour (240 grams)
1¼ cup white whole wheat flour (150 grams)
1½ teaspoons salt
1½ teaspoons honey or sorghum
¼ cup untoasted wheat germ (32 grams)
1½ cup water

Put all ingredients into the bread machine in the order listed and close the lid. You don't need to grease the pan. Set the baking cycle to white bread, set the timer if desired, and turn the machine on. When the bread has finished baking, remove the cylinder and pop out the loaf.

Hook your finger through the hole in the paddle and pull it out.

Let bread cool before slicing it with a serrated knife. The bottom two slices will have indentations from the paddle, but just slice along the paddle line to make them barely noticeable.

Keeps at room temperature for about four days wrapped in a tea towel or a plastic bag, if you can resist eating it before then.

WHAT'S NEXT?

Roger sits across from me at the picnic table, buffing an exaggerated portrait of Hildi that he whittled out of oak. When he chuckles, I look up from my iPad and out through the porch screen to see what he's pointing at. Sylvester the barn cat skulks down the grassy hill behind the house, tail twitching as he stalks a butterfly.

It's all wi-fi and ceiling fan in here, but still the ancient veldt out there.

"Farmer Bee, I'm working on a flyer for the fall CSA season. Where are your stats on how people liked what they got last year? What are you replacing the duds with?"

"Stats? Duds?! Girl, what are you talking about?"

"You know. You give people a big box of food every week What do they gobble up and what gets tossed out?"

"Nothing gets tossed! They all signed the same contract that you did."

I look at him quizzically. "Aren't you the one who said '*Doveryai, no proveryai*'? You surely don't believe everyone takes your contract literally."

"Of course they do. I follow my part to the letter. Why shouldn't they?"

I see a frown forming between his black eyebrows. Uh oh.

"Well, maybe they do. But still. They must like some veg more than others. And maybe they are buying food at the grocery store that you could be growing for them."

"I can see that," he says with the clipped words of a deeply annoyed person.

He goes into the kitchen and comes back with two glasses of chilled white wine. "Philippe at Total Wine thought we'd like this."

"Oh? And how did he know that?"

"He said this Riesling from Shelton Vineyards in the Yadkin Valley was the most popular new whatever at the tasting last week."

"Do you think he keeps track of what people like and orders more?"

"By Bacchus, I get your point! What should we do?"

"Let's do a survey. But people sometimes say one thing and do another. The Senator used to say that the only poll that's really accurate is the one in the voting booth. Let's see how they vote."

"Is that even legal? And how will that help me decide what to plant?"

"Vote for veg, Farmer Bee. We'll offer samples and let them vote with their forks."

"Or without them," he said, picking up the last of the three types of crackers I'd brought over from Charlotte's. "I'm voting a straight Chia-seed ticket."

Chia-Seed Crackers

Active time: 9 minutes. Total time: 20 minutes. Serves 8.

1 clove garlic
2 tablespoons olive oil or canola oil
1 cup white whole wheat flour (120 grams)
2 teaspoons chia seeds
½ teaspoon baking powder
½ teaspoon salt
¼ cup water
coarse salt for sprinkling

Heat oven to 400°F, with a bread stone or a heavy cookie sheet, rim side down, on the bottom rack.

Mince garlic, then heat garlic and oil in a small, microwave-safe container in the microwave on high until oil boils and garlic is fragrant, about 40 seconds.

Put flour, chia seeds, baking powder, and salt into a food processor fitted with the cutting blade. Pulse once or twice to mix, then add garlic and oil. Pulse five or six times until mixture resembles coarse sand.

With the motor running, pour water into the food processor. If flour mixture doesn't come together in a ball within a few seconds, dribble in more water until it does.

Put dough on floured parchment paper. Sprinkle top of dough lightly with flour so it doesn't stick, then cover with another sheet of parchment. Roll out dough using a rolling pin or a flat-sided tall bottle (a clean wine bottle will do) until it is very thin and about the size of a cookie sheet.

Peel off top sheet of parchment. If desired, score dough using a pizza wheel or knife to make break points. Poke each cracker segment all the way through with a fork to keep bubbles from forming during baking. Sprinkle with coarse salt, then use your hand to press it in lightly so it sticks.

Put dough and bottom parchment sheet on a pizza peel or rimless cookie sheet. Slide dough and parchment onto bread stone and bake for 11 minutes, until crackers are tan all over with slightly browner edges and crisp. Cool crackers on a wire rack, then break into pieces. Best eaten within a few hours, but crackers will keep for three or four days in an air-tight container at room temperature.

Variations: For basic crackers to show off toppings, use canola oil without chia seeds or garlic. For spicy crackers, use canola oil and add ½ teaspoon ground chipotle.

STAND BY MY MAN

Folks are already showing up for that famous hippie author y'all got coming today." Nicole says as Roger and I set up the booth. "I don't 'spect there will be anything left for Help the Hungry today."

"Sure will, Doll," says Roger. "Everybody is awash in corn and cukes today. Sophia will help you put a box together before she fetches Ms. Magenta at the hotel."

"Thank *you*, Rog!"

I get an unwanted glimpse at her gym-hardened body as she leans down to scoop corn into her donation box. Doesn't a tank top that flimsy require a shirt over it?

She looks like a beach-volleyball player now, all lean lithe grace. Someday her skin will wrinkle and dry from all that sun exposure, but at twenty-five Nicole is smooth golden perfection.

"We sure do have a herd of heifers at the market today," Nicole says. She gestures with her chin at a trio of grandmotherly women in pastel jogging outfits. Nicole rolls her eyes and tsks with distain.

Bitch! I think. Sure, those women look like they spend more time watching the Food Network than working out, but there's no need to be mean.

Roger frowns. "Miss Price, you surely can't be referring to honored customers of the Midtown Market, the source of your livelihood and mine?"

"Come on, Rog. I'm only kidding," Nicole says with no shame at all. She bites her lip and dips her pointy chin down, looking up through mascaraed lashes. "Forgive me?"

"I will. On one condition. Bring your peach cobbler to the solstice party again this year."

"Done deal. I'll save a dance for you, too."

I turn to see her pat him playfully on the chest and wheel her cart to the next booth, swaying her skinny ass more than usual.

"Solstice party?" I ask, trying to keep my voice from betraying my jealousy. I thought we were a couple now, but clearly Roger has other plans.

"Yeah, Kathy has one every year. We all sit around jawing about crops and politics. Everybody brings a dish. Kathy keeps the lemonade and beer flowing. At sunset, we light a big bonfire and dance while the Wilber brothers play."

This week's band starts up a mournful old-timey tune as Roger turns to answer a question about peaches.

"All free-stone this week, Ma'am."

Potluck-Pride Peach Cobbler

Active time: 20 minutes. Total time: 1 hour. Serves 8.

vegetable oil for baking dish
½ cup sugar (100 grams)
1 tablespoon corn starch
4½ cups peeled, chopped peaches (7 or 8 peaches)

topping
1½ cup Good Baking Mix (180 grams) (page 44)
⅓ cup sugar (66 grams)
⅓ cup water
½ teaspoon vanilla

Heat oven to 400°F. Oil a pretty 8-cup (2 liter) baking dish. In a medium bowl, mix sugar and corn starch. Peel and chop peaches and put into the baking dish. Sprinkle with sugar mixture and toss to mix. Bake until peaches look juicy, about 15 minutes.

Meanwhile, stir together topping ingredients in the medium bowl until just combined and nearly smooth. Drop by the spoonful over hot peach mixture. Bake uncovered for about 35 minutes, until biscuits start to brown and peaches bubble.

Serve warm or at room temperature. Keeps at room temperature for up to four hours. Cover and refrigerate any extra for up to four days.

Nicole wows overnight guests by serving them warm cobbler for breakfast. She reheats two servings in the microwave on high for about a minute.

COSMIC AQUARIUM

Fighting tears, I avoid the concerned looks from the hotel desk clerks and dash up the curved staircase to the elevated lobby that hovers over the welcome desk between the front doors of the Renaissance and its restaurant. Damn that Nicole! And damn Roger for looking at her that way.

Thank heavens the lobby is empty. I sink face down onto a plush couch and sob. How could I compete with *that*? And even if the golden straw of her hair didn't catch his eye, and even if he didn't want to run his tan hand down her bare back into her dangerously low-slung shorts, surely he wanted to kiss her long neck down to her outrageously unfettered breasts below.

Got. To. Get. A. Grip. I clamp down on an outright wail and force my sobs to become whimpers. Still alone! I sit up, wipe my eyes, and look toward the elevator for Alouicious Magenta. I rehearse again how I'll greet the famous chef. Do I dare call her "Allie" like her fans do?

Who cares about Nicole! I got the founder of the farm-to-restaurant movement to add a cooking demonstration at the Bee's Knees booth to her national book tour! I can't believe I'm going to taste Jicama Stars with Ginger-Carrot Puree made by her own hand!

Still two minutes before she's due. I breath in the rich cooking smells from the restaurant below. People stroll in the blazing sunlight outside, down the main street and around the corner to the market, but they can't reach me here. The green carpet cools the searing summer light. Elevated, enclosed by twin handrails, tucked in by a low ceiling, I feel the sudden coziness I loved when I hid on Zia Donatella's stairs to read Nancy Drew books. I close my eyes and relax into that memory.

"Sophia? Why are you crying?" asks a low voice right in front of me. My eyes jerk open. There's Allie within hugging distance. She's resplendent in a sea-green genie outfit, with bejeweled combs in her red curls. She'd come up the stairs as quietly as a reef fish.

"I'm not crying," I say, giving in to the urge to hug her. "Least not anymore." After reading all her books and her warm emails agreeing to do the demonstration, I feel like we're old friends.

"There, there," she whispers, holding me tight. "Tell me what's wrong. We've got time."

She plops down on the sofa and pats the seat next to her, looking genuinely concerned. I find myself telling her how I never expected this rough, wry farmer named Roger to grow so important to my happiness.

"Sometimes he makes me feel beautiful again. Joyous, like a young filly kicking up her heels! But I know my filly days are over. Why should he want me when that young do-gooder is so hot to *intern* for him?"

"Sophia, wild child, your filly days may be over but now you have the strength and wisdom of a mare. Revel in your adult body, twitch your tail, and shake your mane!"

Allie stands up and, taking my hands, pulls me up with her.

"Come on, let's do a little mare dance before we go out there." She gives a soft whinny, winks at me, and begins to prance. I can't help but laugh. We lift our knees high and twitch our rears, pawing the air before us. The mezzanine now seems less like an aquarium than a green pasture.

The elevator dings and she hugs me again as an older couple emerges holding hands.

"See how he looks at her?" Allie asks. "They're eighty-five if they're a day, but he's still got that twinkle. And compared to you, she's a very grey mare."

I wipe tears of laughter from my eyes. "That's what I want."

"Would this help?" Allie holds out a hotel key. "I've got the room for tonight, but I'm grabbing my bags and heading out right after the demo. Why don't you take my extra room key? You and your stallion can come up here to rinse the lather off yourselves after the market. I've even got a coupon for a free appetizer from their new farm-to-fork restaurant."

I grab the key with a big smile. "You're the best! I've been dreaming about coming here!"

Jicama Stars with Ginger-Carrot Puree and Fennel

Active time: 20 minutes. Total time: 20 minutes. Makes about 60 stars and 20 reverse-star garnishes.

2 large carrots
1 tablespoon fresh ginger, baby ginger if available
1 tablespoon coconut milk, apple juice, or water
pinch salt
1 soft-ball sized jicama (about 1 pound or 454 grams)
2 fresh fennel leaves

Cut unpeeled carrots into one-inch sections and microwave in a covered, microwave-safe container on high until very tender, about 4 minutes.

Peel adult ginger or give baby ginger a good scrub. Slice crosswise into thin slices.

Set up a food processor with the cutting blade. Turn machine on high and drop ginger in, letting it bounce and mince. Turn food processor off, then add carrots, coconut milk, and salt. Pulse a few times, scraping down the sides, until mixture is a fairly smooth puree.

Peel jicama, slice in half, then slice crosswise into thin sheets about ⅛th inch thick. Use a small cookie cutter to cut out stars or other shapes. Center your cookie cutter on smaller slices so the remaining outline can be used as a garnish. On larger slices, cut out as many shapes as you can. Arrange stars on serving tray. Save remaining jicama for other uses.

Put carrot puree into a small plastic bag. Cut a small hole in one bottom corner of the bag. Squeeze a dab of carrot puree through the hole onto each jicama star.

Remove fennel leaves from stems, then cut stems into lengths shorter than the stars are wide. Gently press one stem section or tiny spray of fennel leaves into each mound of carrot puree.

Serve at once or keep chilled for a few hours.

RENAISSANCE ROMANCE

The sun beating down makes Allie's portable cooktop practically redundant. You could cook a tortilla on the sidewalk. The *My Carolina Today* crew holds up big light diffuser while Valonda Calloway interviews Allie for a segment on the show next Tuesday. The director tells me that the glare would have made it impossible to see either of them or the Jicama Stars otherwise.

Allie makes the "call me" sign when Roger's not looking, then heads back to the Renaissance Hotel to prep for the next leg of her tour.

It's nearly noon. Most customers have fled back to air-conditioned spaces. Vendors edge their sling chairs further under their tents, following the shrinking rectangles of shade as the sun climbs higher.

We sold out early today, with customers driving for hours just to see Allie. They bought from other booths, too. Mr. Henry, Peg, and a few other vendors stop by to thank us before they head out.

Roger wipes his forehead and neck with a bandana. "Hope it's not this hot for Kathy's Solstice party."

"Whatever."

"Whatever? Sophia, do you have heat stroke?"

"Wouldn't want you and Nicole to get too hot dancing, that's all."

"You're the dancer I'm thinking about. I want you hot, but not too hot to show them Wilber boys how my gal can kick up her heels."

I do a little mental dance right then. Nicole might get a dance out of "Rog," but I'm his gal!

He heaves the last box into the truck and looks at me curiously. "What are you smiling at?"

"There's just one more thing before you go."

"Come on, Sophia, not today. I'm pert' near ready to die from this heat."

"I can fix that — and sooner than you think." I hold up the room key and glance meaningfully toward the hotel. "How about a cold shower, Farmer Bee?"

At the hotel, the porter holds the door for us, his face not registering surprise at our sun-baked appearance or our lack of luggage. We ride up the elevator, still too hot to touch each other even as the cool dry air begins to revive us. Two women rave about the socca they just had in Flights, the hotel restaurant, evidently a to-die-for street treat from Nice.

After the bustle and brightness of the market, the 6th floor is luxuriously subdued.

"Shower!" says Roger gleefully, taking my hand. He leads me through the suite's living room, past a king-sized bed, and into a marble-and-granite bathroom.

I taste salt as he kisses me and pulls my sticky shirt off over my head. He unhooks my bra and we laugh as my breasts cling to its dampness. Soon, all of our clothes are in a damp heap on the tiled floor.

Shampoo foams in my hair as Roger washes away the cares of the morning. He swirls it up on my head in a crown.

He rubs the bar soap until it foams. The fragrance of rosemary and mint fills the shower. He washes my breasts far longer than would be strictly called for by the ServSaf guidelines, then stands back to look at me with undisguised lust in his deep green eyes. We're done talking.

Socca It To Me

Active time: 20 minutes. Total time: 40 minutes. 8 appetizer servings or 4 main-dish servings, perfect for room service.

1 cup chickpea flour (120 grams)
1¼ cup water
1 bunch Swiss chard, about 8 ounces (226 grams)
½ yellow onion
1 tablespoon olive oil
1 teaspoon salt
1 teaspoon freshly ground black pepper

Heat oven to 450°F. Put an oven-proof, well-seasoned or non-stick 9-inch skillet into the oven. Use cast-iron skillet if you have it.

Whisk dry ingredients together in a medium bowl. Add about half the water, whisk until batter is smooth, then stir in remaining water.

Stack chard leaves on your cutting board so stems line up, then make a V-shaped cut to remove the stems from the leaves. (You may need to make two or three stacks.) Cut off and compost the bottom edge of the stems. Chop the rest into pieces about ¼-inch long.

Cut onion half from stem end to root end, then slice crossways as thinly as you can. Pour olive oil in the hot skillet, add chard stems and onion, then stir to coat with oil. Roast in oven until soft, about five minutes.

Cut chard leaves into thin ribbons, about ¼ inch wide. Put a trivet and a fork near the oven. Carefully move the skillet from the oven to the trivet. Stir chard leaves into onion mixture, spread evenly, then pour chickpea batter over vegetables. Use a fork to poke through batter until fork tines touch skillet in about a dozen places to let steam escape. Bake for 15 minutes until top starts to crack and bits of chard and onion begin to brown. Then broil for about 3 minutes more until socca is brown in spots and the edges are crispy.

Cut socca into wedges and serve hot or warm. Refrigerate extra for a day or two. Reheat in a toaster oven.

SUMMER SOLSTICE

W hy are you stopping?" I ask as Roger pulls his pickup into a dark turnaround on the moonlit lane leading from Kathy's farm to the highway.

"Tailgate party." He reaches behind his seat to pull out a gym bag. "Meet me behind the truck."

I set the covered dish that had held quinoa salad down on the floor in front of me. I open the heavy door and step carefully into knee-high wild flowers. A branch catches my black curls, wild from dancing around the bonfire at Kathy's celebration. Drums and laughter drift through the woods, but it is too far away to hear the crackling of the flames.

I do hear a zipper. I flush with anticipation, but something is wrong. I am well acquainted by now with the sound of the zipper opening on Roger's jeans. This sounded too sturdy, too long. As my eyes adjust to the dark after the glare of the headlights, I see him pull a soft quilt out of the gym bag and spread it in the truck bed.

Roger unlatches the tailgate, then lifts me up in a spinning embrace that ends with my bottom bouncing on the tailgate. He tugs off my sandals.

"Put your arms behind you and lift up your hips," he says. I lean and lift, the cool metal welcome against my hot thighs. He slides down my new lacy thong and sets it next to my sandals in the corner of the truck.

"Scooch back," he says in a husky voice. I put my heels up on the truck and crab backward into the truck. Not graceful, but quick. No time for ladylike behavior now.

I hear his more familiar zipper come down amid a chorus of cicadas and tree frogs. Lighting bugs flicker on and off in the clearing and a multitude of stars flicker above, with no city lights or smog to dim them.

"You looked so hot dancing around the fire," he says as he scrabbles up between my open thighs. "You make me too crazy to drive."

He kisses me long and deep. I arch against him, then lift my head to get a glimpse of his bare ass in the moonlight. It is one fine ass indeed.

I close my eyes and wrap myself around him. Two dancers in a rocking truck, making our own fire on the longest day of the year.

Quinoa Salad with Chioggia Beets

Active time: 20 minutes, starting with cooked chickpeas (page). Total time: 30 minutes. Makes 4 main-dish servings or 8 sides.

4 small beets (save any beet greens for another recipe)
1 cup quinoa (170 grams)
1⅓ cup water
½ teaspoon salt
1 cucumber (about 1 cup chopped)
1 bell pepper
1½ cups cooked chickpeas (250 grams or one 15-ounce can)
½ cup chickpea broth, apple juice, or water

Scrub beets and pierce several times with a fork and put in a covered, microwave-safe container. Microwave on high for 5 minutes. Turn beets over and microwave until they are fork-tender, about 5 minutes more. Uncover and let cool so you can peel them.

Put quinoa, water, and salt in a medium pot, cover, and bring to a boil over high heat. Reduce heat to low so water barely boils and cook covered for 15 minutes. Turn off the heat and, without lifting the lid, let quinoa finish steaming for 5 minutes.

Meanwhile, cut slices off both ends of the cucumber and taste, then peel if bitter. Cut cucumber and pepper into bite-sized pieces. Put vegetables into a non-absorbent serving or storage container as you go. For example, a glass bowl shows off the colors and won't stain.

Cut off stem and root ends of beets and compost. Peel beets and cut into bite-sized pieces, saving beet juice.

Fluff quinoa with a fork. Toss with chickpeas and vegetables, then drizzle with any beet juice and about half the chickpea broth to deepen the flavor and help the salad stick together a bit for easier eating. Use apple juice or water if you are using canned chickpeas. Toss again until beets turn the quinoa pink, taste, and add salt or more chickpea broth if desired.

Serve at room temperature or chilled. Keeps refrigerated for 5 days.

MELONS

I lay bare-assed across Roger's knee, chin pressed against a rough bale of straw. Cantaloupes stretch as far as I can see in the hot August sun. Their big leaves would cover me, I think. But do I want to be covered?

"You like this, you little Vixen?" Roger growls above me, stroking my stinging red curves with his work-roughened hand. "Tell me you do. Say it or I won't give you more. Ask me for more."

I struggle to free my hands from his tight grasp behind my back. Someone else — another woman! — says "More, please!" Who can be out here in the fields witnessing my shame and delight? What right does she have to ask Roger to spank me?

I jerk awake.

"More tomatoes, please," Jo Lynn is saying. "Roger, you know that just three pounds won't make near enough gazpacho!"

I blink and look around. I've dozed off at the market, slumped in a lawn chair. My hand rests on a sun-lit cantaloupe. I pull my hand and the box of melons back into the scant shade of the white tent. Sweat trickles between my breasts, as unwelcomed as a tired cliché. This was day ten of a heat wave and I am exhausted.

"Hey there, Sleepy Head," says Jo Lynn. "You two need any help for the farm tour next week? I'd be happy to gussy up your barn."

"Thanks, Jo Lynn, but the folks come out for kittens and corn, not the decor," Roger says, laughing.

I'm quiet, still caught up in my dream. Charlotte's mock-shocked chatter last night about some trashy book she'd been reading must have stuck in a primitive part of my mind.

Roger's never been violent with me. Driven, even rough once we got started, but never ouch-making. Kenny and I had tried that kind of play a few times after watching a spicy movie, but always dissolved in laughter.

Roger's tee has a triangle of sweat between his shoulder blades, running down to the base of his spine. His market jeans are clean and worn, made lighter by rigorous farm work.

I do want more, but not like that. I want to subscribe, not submit. Even be a little domesticated, but not dominated. I remember Roger zipping up my beekeeper's hood to protect me from bee stings. It's impossible to imagine him wanting to flog me, even if I begged him to. Whatever works for consenting adults is NOMB, but I'll take CSA over BDSM any day.

Roger cuts Navaho Purple tomatoes for samples, but pauses as I stretch and stand up. He winks at me and speaks low, so the customers filling their bags won't hear.

"Wait 'til I get you home. I've got some samples that will curl your toes."

"I bet you do, Farmer Bee!" And I know the only reason I'll be wearing long sleeves this week will be to protect against blackberry brambles, not to hide bruises and welts.

Cantaloupe and Blackberry Salad

Active time: 10 minutes. Total time: 10 minutes. Serves 8 to 12.

12 ounces ripe blackberries (about 340 grams)
1 medium cantaloupe
mint leaves (optional)
Cashew Cream (page 90) (optional)

The exact quantity of fruit for the recipe matters far less than the ripeness of the fruit. The blackberries should be plump and dull black, not shiny, reddish, or green. The cantaloupe should be golden, not green, heavy for its size, fragrant, and have a stem button that gives slightly when pressed.

Set a strainer over a bowl. Scrub cantaloupe with soap and water and rinse well before cutting. Cut it in half and put goop and seeds into the strainer to drain. Drink juice or use it to sweeten iced tea.

Cut cantaloupe halves into wedges about a half-inch wide at the widest part. Cut between orange flesh and rind, then leave fruit in place while you cut crosswise to make bite-sized pieces. Heap melon in a beautiful bowl or, if serving soon, individual bowls.

Rinse blackberries and pull or cut out any hulls, then put on top of melon. Top with a few mint leaves and Cashew Cream if desired.

Enjoy chilled after a steamy workout.

RESULTS

I weigh the last bowl of cherry tomatoes and update my spreadsheet. Just as I'd suspected, the Yellow Pear Tomato, one of the oldest of the heirloom types, did better the second week. Only the kids liked the red Supersweet 100s better.

Every week, I put out four sample plates. Two were different varies of a new fruit or vegetable and one was a repeat of the last week's samples. That way, I could see if the winner from one week would get "re-elected." Turned out that as in politics, people went for looks the first time, but were loyal to the choice that did something for them. In this case, the job was to taste good.

"Would you like an easy recipe to dress these up?" I ask a mom who stops by, holding out a flyer. "They're good raw, but you can make them fancy in five minutes."

"Thanks! I love free recipes." She takes the recipe card then takes another quart of cherry tomatoes.

"Then you might want to sign up for our newsletter," I say, handing her the clipboard. I hear Roger chuckling behind me as she walks away.

"Dang, Sorghum, you really know how to work a booth."

"It's no big secret, Farmer Bee. I'm just letting them know about the amazing food you've grown."

"Know and taste. I've grown those Navaho Purples for years. Most people won't touch them. Too dark, might be spoiled! Pure genius to put them on a plate with those old comforting red Mortgage Lifters."

"We're down to our last box of tomatoes and it's still only ten thirty."

"Sorghum, you've set a record!" Roger says, patting me on the back. His hand lingers and drops down to my waist. "That wraps it. I'm going to a conference at Warren Wilson College next Saturday. You're in charge next week."

"At my usual rate?"

"Of course. Just make sure you don't give it all out as samples."

Sautéed Cherry Tomatoes

Active time: 5 minutes. Total time: 5 minutes. Serves 2.

1 garlic clove
1 cup cherry tomatoes
1 teaspoon olive oil

Mince garlic and set aside. Rinse cherry tomatoes and towel-dry to avoid splatters when the water and hot oil interact.
Heat olive oil in a medium skillet over medium heat. When oil is hot, add garlic, stir once, then add tomatoes. Cook, stirring frequently, until tomatoes are warmed through and a few start to split, about 2 minutes.

Serve hot or at room temperature as a side dish or tossed with hot angel-hair pasta. Note that unsplit tomatoes straight from the skillet can feel quite hot when they burst in your mouth.

QUEEN OF THE BOOTH

Minutes before the market opens the next week, I'm arranging and re-arranging vegetables as if Martha Stewart her own bad self might show up with a camera crew.

When I went by to pick up the produce last night, Roger thanked me thoroughly for tending the booth while he's at a conference today. *Molto bene!* I stretch luxuriously up toward the tent. My skirt, loose now in the waist, falls further down my hips. Are low riders still in style?

I shift a basket of garlic back next to the artful pyramid of baby squash and take a picture of lush bundles of mint, rosemary, and chives tied with twine. Just as I zap it up to our Facebook page, the first customers approach.

Oh no. It's Sally Johnson and Ruth Carter with their herd of brats. I brace myself as they push their strollers up to the booth.

"Nice morning," Sally said. "Glad the rain stopped around midnight last night."

"Very nice," I agree, looking over their shoulders for other customers to rescue me. I noticed their entries in Roger's account book last night. Now I know why she'd mentioned "settling up" when I first met her. Neither family had paid for their spring CSA subscriptions — and the Johnsons hadn't paid for their winter one either. Yet each week they took full-share boxes and more. Between the two of them, they owed Bee's Knees Farm over $2000.

I'd flashed back to my frustration during the Senator's staff meetings, when his treasurer ticked through the list of outstanding pledges. I remembered how Mamma worked a second job every Christmas to make sure we met our obligations.

If Roger didn't have the nerve to get these women to play fair, then I'd do it. I wasn't about to get laid off again because of freeloaders.

Sure enough, both women bag up green beans, okra, summer squash, and cantaloupes. One of their little hoodlums grabs at the

Thai basil, attracted by the purple flowers atop the green leaves. The friends laugh and take two bunches of basil each.

"Where's Roger?"

"He's up near Ashville this week. I'm in charge today."

"Whoo-whee! He's never left this to anyone else. He must like you a lot." Sally elbows Ruth in the side and both mothers chuckle.

"I guess he told you to weigh this up then and note it in his book."

I clear my throat and look her straight in her pale gray eyes. "No, he didn't mention you at all. What he *did* say was to not give everything away. This isn't a charity."

Sally blinks and swallows. Ruth takes a half-step back and reaches for the hand of a three-year-old in an old-fashioned sunbonnet.

"But we've got an arrangement," Sally said. "I told you before, we're going to settle up soon."

"I'm working with Roger on the business now. Like I said, he didn't mention any 'arrangement.' I'm happy to sell you any food you can pay for. Otherwise, please step aside and let these other customers in."

Sally and Ruth look at each other with astonishment. Ruth seems to be blinking back tears, but I just wave over their shoulders to the Hardisons, who are coming up to the booth. Have I gone too far? I thought they'd just go to the ATM and settle up.

"Come on, Ruth," says Sally. "Let's not make a scene. Give Roger's new friend all that stuff back and we'll go to Wal-Mart."

One of the toddlers starts to wail as Sally wrests a bouquet of basil from his grubby little paws, but they clear out just as Mary Beth Hardison starts asking about the difference between the three types of snap beans we have this week.

One-Pot Barely Cooked Tomato Sauce with Noodles
Active time: 10 minutes. Total time: 25 minutes. 4 servings.

2 garlic cloves
¼ teaspoon olive oil
1 cup chopped spring onions
2 pounds ripe tomatoes
¼ teaspoon ground chipotle
2 teaspoons fresh or 1 teaspoon dried oregano
1¼ cup whole-wheat rotini or other short noodles
¼ cup fresh basil leaves, cut into thin ribbons
optional topping: ½ cup shelled hemp seeds or nutritional yeast
(nooch)

Mince garlic and set aside. Spread olive oil in a medium pot
and turn heat on medium low. Add chopped spring onions to the
pot, stirring occasionally to prevent burning.

Chop tomatoes, making sure to cut tomato skin into pieces an
inch across or less. Add garlic and chipotle to pot, stir once, and
then add chopped tomatoes, oregano, and rotini. Stir to mix, then
use a ladle to push noodles down into the tomato mixture as much
as possible. Don't worry if some stick up above tomatoes. Cover the
pot and bring tomato mixture to a boil over high heat, then reduce
heat to medium low, so sauce barely boils.

Simmer pasta about 12 minutes until tender. It will take 2 or
3 minutes longer to cook in tomato juice than in does in water.
Every few minutes, stir noodles and sauce, then push the noodles
down into the liquid. As tomatoes release their juice, noodles will
increasingly be submerged. Toward the end of the cooking time,
bite a noodle every minute or so until your test shows that they are
firm but cooked through.

Ladle pasta and sauce into bowls and top with basil ribbons
and either nutritional yeast or hemp seeds for extra flavor and nutri-
tion. Any extra will keep for about four days refrigerated.

POT OF GOLD

Crepe myrtles bloom along the edge of the highway, deep pink and white against the dark green pines as I drive out to Bee's Knees Farm on Tuesday.

I reach down to turn up the car radio just before the long bridge over Jordan Lake, singing along with the Carolina Chocolate Drops about cornbread and butterbeans.

Twenty minutes later, I flip open the cash box with a big sweep of my arm. "Ta da!" I rejoice to Roger. "Best week since you started keeping this notebook! We sold completely out!"

"Way to go, Saleswoman Sophia! I'll have to go away more often and leave you in charge." He pulls me close and kisses me until I feel a throb of energy from my knees all the way through my body to his insistent mouth. I want more, but he breaks away and picks up the worn spiral-ring notebook.

"Jumping juniper berries, you did sell a lot! I didn't think I'd given you that much to work with. Are you sure you weren't dancing for tips?"

"You mean like this?" I say, doing a little clog dance to the fiddle music echoing in my head.

"Per-zactly like that," he says, kissing me again.

"Nope, I'm a private dancer. I just used a business practice you seem to not have heard of. I sold goods for money."

He looks puzzled. "What's new about that?"

"I *sold* all of it. Two moochers came by again looking for a handout. I told them to pay cash or be gone."

"Moochers? I've never seen anyone mooching at Midtown."

"You old softie! I mean those women with all their kids. The ones who owe you thousands of dollars. They each wanted your weekly donation of fifty dollars, but I stood up to them." I pat the accounts book, waiting for him to absorb my accomplishment.

"You mean Sally and Ruth? The Johnsons and the Carters? They're good, honest people."

"Good, honest people who can afford cell phones but claim not to have the money to pay you for food you worked so hard to grow! Roger, I'm perfectly happy to play the bad cop here if that's what it takes to make the farm succeed."

Roger frowns and clenches his fists, green eyes stormy. "You thoughtless, cruel woman. What have you done? The Johnsons and the Carters are why I even have this farm! Sally's daddy Ralph showed me how to grow something other than bricks in red clay. And Ruth is married to Ben Carter's oldest boy. Ben got me through the tomato blight two years ago. I've eaten at their tables and played with their kids for ages."

"What have *I* done? Exactly what you told me too. You said not to give everything away. *Why didn't you tell me?*"

The dogs, hearing our anger, whine in distress.

"I'm not *giving it away*. They're going to pay me when they can. But by Thor's hammer, woman, they're on hard times now. Both families lost their farms when the new highway went through. Now they're in the city, applying for food stamps. This after generations of feeding others. They're trying to make a go of working for someone else after being leaders in the farming community. Ruth has even taken in her sister's kids while she's overseas with the National Guard. And you're calling them *moochers* and taking food out of the mouths of their children!"

Roger glowers at me while he makes a quick phone call. "Sally, Roger here. I'm sorry beyond sorry about the mix-up this weekend. You going to be home in an hour? Good, stay put. I'll be by with something for dinner and more."

He hang up and punches another number. "Ruth, Roger here. Sorry about …"

I slink out.

Chocolate Crows

Active time: 15 minutes. Total time: 1 hour. Makes about 36 crows, enough for 12 happy people or one very sad person.

3.5 ounces 90% cocoa chocolate (such as Lindt's Excellence Supreme Dark bars) (100 grams)
¾ cup sorghum (500 grams)
1 cup pecans halves (340 grams or 4 ounces)
3 cups dried, unsweetened coconut (200 grams or 7 ounces)
sprinkling of coarse salt, optional

Break chocolate bar into squares and put into a 2-quart micro-wave-safe bowl. Microwave on high for about 2½ minutes, stirring every 30 seconds, until chocolate is melted. Stir in sorghum until mixture is glossy, for about 30 seconds.

Line a cookie sheet with parchment or waxed paper.

Chop pecans coarsely into pieces about the size of a split pea. Stir pecans and coconut into chocolate mixture. Drop by the tea-spoonful onto the cookie sheet in truffle-size clumps that that look like crows if you squint. Sprinkle tails with a few grains each coarse salt if desired. Chill until firm if you have the will power, about 45 minutes. Eat while still cold or the chocolate will melt. Keeps refrigerated in a sealed container for longer than they last.

STUNNED BY GOOGLE

What have I done? It's bad enough that Roger is this mad at me. But to have possibly caused those kids I called brats to go to bed hungry?

Just before the Jordan Lake bridge, I swerve off the road to park in a spot favored by birders looking for the bald eagles who nest nearby. I pull Flicka out of my purse and ask her to find the background of the two families who'd helped Roger.

From very bad to worse: Ralph Johnson was one of the first people named Farmer of the Year by the Carolina Farm Stewardship Association "for his stellar support of young farmers." Ben and Betty Carter had won the following year "for their generous sharing of sustainable growing techniques." Glowing testimonials for both families describe how they welcomed new techniques and young farmers into the area while sharing their deep love of the land.

The Johnsons had even worked out an exchange program with the Amish who still used horses to pull plows. Tears filled my eyes as I watch a video showing a much younger Sally being lifted up by her daddy onto the back of a big Belgian plough horse during a farm tour.

I find Sally's Facebook page and bite my lip in despair. Yes, her sister Brittany is in Afghanistan — in a military hospital recovering from an encounter with an IED.

I follow a comment link to Ruth's page. Her status updates are determinedly upbeat. She "likes" that her brother-in-law Henry had another job interview today, even if he's worried that his unemployment benefits will run out. Looks like he's another victim of the merger between Duke Power and Progress Energy.

I walk out to look at the sun setting over the lake. An eagle flies along the shoreline, bringing flustered quacks from a flock of ducks settling in for the night. A sliver of moon peeks up over the trees on the eastern shore.

What can I do to make this right?

Two hours later, I'm in my kitchen with a plan and my Zia Donatella's recipe box. I will make the soup she used to bring over after Papà left.

Core Recipe: Bonus Broth

Active time: 10 minutes. Total time: 4 to 8 hours. Yield: 6½ cups broth and 5 cups cooked chickpeas.

2 cups dried chickpeas (400 grams)
2 carrots, scrubbed but unpeeled
2 yellow onions, unpeeled
4 garlic cloves, rinsed but unpeeled
12 cups water
1 tablespoon salt

Pick over chickpeas, removing any stones or non-chickpea items. Rinse well and put in a slow cooker.

Cut carrots into quarters across and then lengthwise, then put in the slow cooker. Remove any really dirty parts of the onion peel. Rinse onions and trim off their root ends, then cut them in half from stem to root. Put onions, garlic, water, and salt into the slow cooker. Cover slow cooker and cook on high for about four hours or on low for about eight hours, until chickpeas are tender.

Lift out vegetables and save for Bonus Hummus (page 126) or Stoup (page 83). Pour broth through a strainer. Pick out any remaining vegetable bits from the chickpeas.

Serve hot broth in a beautiful bowl with a few circles of spring onion floating on top. Breath in the steamy fragrance and feel grateful for what you have and what you can give.

APOLOGY

From: Sophia Verde
Subject: Groveling apology. What can this worm do?
Date: July 11, 2012 16:42
To: Roger Branch

Dear Roger,
I'm so utterly sorry that I didn't let Sally and Ruth have their vegetables as usual. I overstepped my bounds in a big way.

Next time, if you'll let me have a next time, I'll check with you
before implementing a new policy like this.

On the other hand, what else haven't you told me?

Yours most contritely and curiously,

Sophia "The Worm" Verde

From: Roger Branch
Subject: Don't Insult Worms
Date: July 11, 2012 21:16
To: Sophia Verde

Dear Not-Worm,

Worms work together to turn spent plants into rich soil. You are
not a worm.

If you think this is a matter of policy and hierarchy, there's no hope for you. If you can see it as a matter of withholding kindness and trust, then we can talk.

Go read Wendell Berry's *Bringing it to the Table* while I cool down.

Disappointed but hopeful,
Roger Branch,
Community Supported Farmer

From: Sophia Verde
Subject: Still ashamed but smarter. Here's a plan.
Date: July 12, 2012 09:56
To: Roger Branch

Dear Roger,

Trust? You could have avoided this whole mess if you'd just told me they were on a payment plan. I'm surprised your accountant hasn't wacked you across the knuckles for not showing that better in your books.

On the other hand, thanks for introducing me to Wendell Berry. Why didn't we read him in high school instead of *Tess of the D'Urbervilles*?

I've written notes of apology to Sally and Ruth. Ruth's brother-in-law may be able to land a job at the farm incubator the Senator cut the ribbon for last week. Hope that works out. Sally and Ruth may not ever forgive me, but at least it's something.

I'll add some Berry quotes to your website, if you'll let me, and promise to look deeper before I let old wounds influence my current actions. Please help me understand more about the farm's history, too. This is so different from the money-is-all, fifty-per-cent-plus-one world I come from. Different and better.

Seeking a second chance,
Sophia "Budding Community Member" Verde

From: Roger Branch
Subject: Second Change Granted
Date: July 12, 2012 19:02
To: Sophia Verde

Dear Seeker,

I've swum with the corporate sharks too, believe it or not, and know that bottom-line bullies often rise to the top. It's hard to break the habit of valuing everything only in terms of quarterly profits.

And I'll admit: I've been burned by over-sharing. I'm not much of one for talking, particularly about hard times. I should have let you know what I would have told any intern left in charge of the booth. Sorry.

Don't glamorize farming too much: we're still in business. It's not all kumbaya out here in the sticks. It would be much better if Chip hadn't been laid off after fifteen years of hard work and if J.P had decent veterans' benefits.

We can't do everything by helping each other out but we do what we can. And we do it directly, without having to compromise with committees or bosses. We give people who want organic food and good conditions for farm workers and animals a chance to vote with their wallets. No need to wait for elections and then pray that your representative represents *you*, not his biggest donor.

Don't feel too guilty. Sally rustled up enough food so everyone had enough to eat until I brought more. They appreciated your notes, even if their feathers are still a little ruffled. They might even be willing to be friends, especially if Chip lands that job. Thanks for setting that up.

Good job on the Berry quotes. Maybe there's hope for both of us yet.

See you at the market Saturday.
Roger Branch,
A Gentleman Farmer Who Never Tells

I smile and go whip up another Donatella special. Her super-thrifty, richly flavored hummus. It's quick and nearly free, a bonus for my budget.

Bonus Hummus

Active time: 8 minutes. Makes 8 servings, ½ cup each.

4 cups cooked chickpeas from making Bonus Broth (page 121)
(650 grams)
⅓ cup Bonus Broth
All the vegetables from making Bonus Broth except onion and
garlic peels
½ cup tahini (120 grams)
⅓ cup olive oil (70 grams)
juice and zest from 2 lemons
2 teaspoons ground cumin
1½ teaspoon salt
½ teaspoon ground chipotle or to taste
black pepper to taste

Set up your food processor with the cutting blade or use a
blender. Add all ingredients and process until smooth. (If you have
a small blender, process the ingredients in batches, then stir to
blend in a storage container or bowl.)

Taste and adjust seasonings. If it tastes right but is just too thick,
add more Bonus Broth.

Serve hot, at room temperature, or chilled. Keeps refrigerated
for four days or frozen for a year.

Where are your prancing ways today, Sophie?," asks Mr. Henry as I pass the old farmer's booth. "Here, try a fig to take your mind off your troubles."

"Thank you, Mr. Henry." I'm as grateful for the delay in facing Roger as I am for the luxuriously ripe fruit. I close my eyes to savor the deep sweetness, as close to chocolate as you can pick off a tree. Each fruit is different, so much more interesting than the square fig cookies that Mamma used to tuck into my lunchbox.

"So good, Mr. Henry!"

"Stop by after the market's over, hon. If there's any left, I'll give you a pint to take home. Some daylilies, too. Look at them all day, then eat the flowers tonight. Now get to work."

"You're the best, Mr. Henry!" Fortified, I make myself walk briskly toward the Bee's Knees booth. Roger must have come early. All the boxes are unpacked and he's setting up the displays. No need for me today.

"There you are, Sorghum!" says Roger. "I thought you'd never get here."

"It's only 7:30. The market doesn't open for another half hour."

"Just enough time to have you arrange everything here. Is this how you set up the boxes?"

"Not quite," I say, angling the boxes and boards that I brought to make shelves. "If you stack them like this, you get three levels. Then even if there's a crowd at the booth, passers-by can see what you've got."

He helps me drape the yellow-and-white checked oilcloth over the shelves. I focus on the work at hand, avoiding his eyes. I'm still so embarrassed by the trouble I caused last week, when I was in charge, and still miffed at Roger's reaction.

"Most colorful and popular items on top, near the cash box." I say. "Lure folks into the booth so they'll see and buy the other stuff you have."

"Like the grocery stores putting milk and beer at the back?"

"Exactly."

I can feel him stare at me as I fuss unnecessarily with the arrangements. Everything looks fine now, more than fine. It looks ready for a *Southern Living* magazine photo shoot.

"Sophia, quit messing with that basil and look at me." I turn toward Roger, still not meeting his gaze. If I were the *Southern Living* art director, I'd make sure Roger was in the pictures too. He's the very vision of a hunky man of the land.

Finally, I look into his eyes. They're a placed sea green today, not stormy like they were last Saturday. His generous mouth turns up into the faintest of smiles and he opens his arms.

"Come here, Sorghum. Let's make up." Roger wraps his arms around me. I lean my cheek against his chest, feeling his heart beat.

"I'm so sorry!"

"Well, I'm sorry I didn't tell you. I forget sometimes that you can't read my mind. That you're used to doing it all by numbers and the bottom line. Sally and Ruth understand, even though you gave them a few rough days. And Chip starts his new job next week.

"*We* gave them a few rough days."

Roger starts to answer, but before he gets a chance, Peg calls out "Kids, get a room or start selling! You're scaring the customers away." I jerk out of Roger's embrace and see Peg cackling over at the Eden Farm booth, grinning from ear to ear.

"Good idea, Peg" Roger calls back to her, then whispers to me "Let's sell this stuff and go see if the rumors about make-up sex are true."

My cheeks flush pink and I swear my heart skips a beat as I turn to face the first wave of customers. If we sell out early, can we leave early? I'm eager to put those rumors to the test.

Daylily Summer-Squash Skillet

Active time: 10 minutes. Total time: 20 minutes. Serves 4.

1 sweet Vidalia-style onion
¼ teaspoon olive oil
4 small summer squash
4 small daylily flowers
4 large daylily flowers

Chop onion. Coat the inside of a medium skillet with olive oil using clean fingers or a brush. Cook onion over medium-low heat in the skillet until it begins to soften, about 4 minutes.

Cut blossom and stem ends off summer squash, then cut squash lengthwise into quarters and across into ¼-inch wedges. Add squash to onions and continue cooking uncovered until vegetables are thoroughly tender but not mushy, about 8 minutes.

Gently rinse daylilies, liberating any ants that may be hiding. Set small flowers aside for garnish. Cut large flowers crossways into half-inch strips. Stir into squash mixture and cook until petals relax, about thirty seconds.

Serve hot, garnished at the last minute with small daylilies.

MAILBOX

I flip through my mail hopefully as always. Surely with all those interviews I'd been going to, an offer letter would appear soon. I see two bills and an envelope full of coupons for stuff I can't afford, even at a discount. Mamma sent a thank-you note for the hand-painted silk scarf I gave her for her birthday plus a wedding announcement for the *daughter* of a girl I knew in high school. Ouch.

Roger pays me to do his outreach and help at the booth, but that is still a very part-time job. My emergency fund is having its own emergency. Next week, my unemployment benefits stop. And if Mamma's clippings are to be trusted, I'm too old to get married but too young for Social Security.

I shrug and check my email, glad I'm not a quivering virgin any more. If I'd married my highschool sweetheart like Mamma wanted, I'd be stuck with him and five kids, working at the Canton papermill.

No good news in my inbox, either, just a canceled interview and an automatic withdrawal for my phone bill. A note from Poll-Pulse thanks me for coming in for the second round of interviews last week. They hired "a more qualified candidate" but will keep my resume on file. *Merda!* At least they didn't leave me dangling, like so many other companies do these days.

I want something sweet and thrifty. How about a version of that Poor Man's Pudding Cake that we used to get on vacation in Quebec, but made with sorghum? I can add one of the first August apples for color, flavor, and some hint of healthiness. Instead of *Pouding Chomeur*, let's call it ... Saving-Up Sorghum Cake.

Saving-Up Sorghum Cake

Active time: 15 minutes. Total time: 45 minutes. Serves 6.

½ cup sorghum
2 teaspoons vinegar
1 large apple
1½ cup Good Baking Mix (180 grams) (page 44)
⅓ cup sugar (66 grams)
2 tablespoons finely ground flaxseed
1 teaspoon cinnamon
½ cup water

Heat oven to 350°F. Pour sorghum and vinegar into an 8 x 8-inch pan and stir to blend. Core and dice apple, then sprinkle evenly over sorghum mixture.

In a medium bowl, stir together dry ingredients, then stir in water until batter is barely mixed but no dry parts remain. Drop batter by the spoonful over the apples so they are nearly covered.

Bake for 30 minutes. Serve hot or at room temperature, turning each serving over as you plate it so the sorghum and apples are on top.

THE OFFER

I check for email responses to the Bee's Knees newsletter, update the farm's Facebook page, and send out a pre-market tweet. Not bad for before 7 o'clock in the morning!

It was too early for the Butler Shuttler, so I walk across Six Forks Road to the market. Peg flags me down as I walk by the Eden Farm booth.

"Sophia, you got a minute? I want to pick your brain."

"Sure, Peg. What's up?"

"I've been noticing what you've been doing for Roger. and I don't mean all that carryin' on and courting right in broad daylight. My girl tells me you've got a website up for him. Facebook and everything And a sign-up sheet to remind folks to come buy it fresh instead of at some big box store."

"No biggie."

"Well, it's a biggie if you don't even like to check email. You're bringing in new customers for the whole market, really."

I nod, proud that we now had a waiting list for the fall CSA.

"Pete and I are just too dog-gone beat to even turn on the computer after working out all day in the fields. I get to it a couple times a week, but that's just not enough any more. Do you think you could help us out?"

"Peg, I don't know ..."

"I'm thinking that just a few hours a week of your time might help make the difference. And we'd pay you, of course."

"If you put it that way, let's talk!"

At lunch, I make my new favorite cheery sandwich: bright yellow lentil spread on toasted Good Whisk Bread, topped with grated carrots, purple cabbage, and thinly sliced purple onion.

Lentilicious Sunshine Spread

Active time: 10 minutes. Total time: 90 minutes. Makes 3 cups.

2 garlic cloves, minced
1 cup red lentils
2 cups water
¼ cup tahini
1 teaspoon ground cumin
1 teaspoon salt
¼ teaspoon turmeric or squirt of yellow prepared mustard
¼ teaspoon ground chipotle or cayenne
1 lemon, juice and zest

Put all ingredients except lemon in a slow cooker. Cover and cook until lentils fall apart, about 90 minutes on high or three hours on low (Slow cookers vary a lot, but it's hard to overcook this recipe.) The lentils naturally change color from orange-red to yellow.

Stir lemon juice and zest into lentils. Taste and adjust seasonings. It thickens as it cools.

Serve Lentilicious Sunshine Spread as you would hummus: hot on baked potatoes or roasted vegetables, at room temperature or chilled as a spread in sandwiches or wraps, and at any temperature as a dip. Keeps in the refrigerator for a week or frozen for a year.

OVERALLS IN THE BARN

I wake up when Hildi squeals at Gullin, snuggling back against Roger. When the potbellied pigs quiet down, all is quiet on the farm. I think back to earlier this afternoon and how we came to be dozing in a pile of clean hay.

Sunlight streaked through the big window in the hayloft to caress Roger's shoulder as he put the pitchfork back between the carved oak pegs that held it against the rough board walls. I wanted to put my hand on his bare shoulder blade, to feel the sun's warmth and his heat rising beneath it.

I lingered in the doorway, admiring how his overalls hung from his shoulders. So hot! The bright sunlight and deep sheltering shade made a chiaroscuro scene, reminding me of the Artemision bronze of Zeus I'd seen one morning during my semester abroad. Roger's deeply cut muscles flex as he lifts the pitchfork up, in, and then down between the pegs.

Lust pulled me forward as the sunlight and shadow call out his thick salt-and-pepper chest hair. *Molto sexy! Who would ever think you could look like that without years of Pilates!* Roger turned. His well-developed pecs looked powerful above his taut waist. Damn those overalls.

My lips parted with desire as I considered the rough denim straps. How they hung off those strong shoulders. Oh my! I wanted to run to him, to lift each burnished loop over its matching button and free the straps so his overalls dropped to his feet.

"Barn cat got your tongue?" he grinned wickedly, running his tanned thumb under the bib hiding his six-pack abs. Emerald eyes blazed into mine. "What are you thinking?"

"Um, how do those overalls work?" I ask, batting my eyes up at him. "I've seen them on Sesame Street, but never on a live person."

"Are you asking if we farmers wear them like the Scots wear their kilts?"

I blushed apple red and felt my deepest muscles clench. "I hear fresh air is healthy."

"Come here and I'll show you just how healthy it can be."

My hiking boots crunched across the straw on the floor. I reached up and placed my bare hands on his shoulders. The one in shadow was warm but the late afternoon sun made the other hotter. Heat radiated up my arms, through my breasts and down my spine to create a swirling fever at my core. Everything else in the world dropped away.

I freed the left strap. His overalls hung now at a slant from one sun-glazed shoulder.

Roger's grin was gone. He'd become as focused as Zeus must have been just before he sired Aphrodite. I freed the other strap and let the soft, work-worn denim puddle at his feet.

Commando! I gasped, dropping to my knees on the warm soft fabric. *And hung indeed.*

Core recipe: Supremely Easy Pizza Sauce

Active time: 2 minutes. Total time: 2 minutes. Tops 3 large pizzas.

one 32-ounce can crushed tomatoes
2 garlic cloves
½ teaspoon oregano
¼ teaspoon chipotle
2 teaspoons olive oil (optional)

Open can. Mince garlic very finely or put it through a garlic press right into the can. Stir in remaining ingredients. Keeps refrigerated for a least a week and freezes well.

Royal Eastern Delight Pizza

Active time: 25. Total time: 40. Makes 1 large pizza with about 12 slices.

2 long, purple Asian eggplants
Dough for one pizza, such as the no-knead Whisk Pizza Dough in *Wildly Affordable Organic*
1 cup Bonus Hummus (page 126)
1½ cup Supremely Easy Pizza Sauce (see above)
1 small purple onion, quartered and cut into thin slices
handful of fresh basil leaves

Heat oven to 450°F with a bread stone or a heavy cookie sheet, rim side down, on the bottom rack.

Use a sharp knife or vegetable peeler to peel eggplant, then cut into half-inch cubes. Put eggplant into a microwave-safe container, cover, and cook on high for about five minutes. Let it rest undisturbed for at least two minutes.

Roll out pizza dough between two well-floured sheets of parchment paper. Peel off top piece of parchment and spread hummus evenly over dough. Spread pizza sauce over hummus.

Stir eggplant and test a few cubes for doneness. They should all be fork-tender. If you're not sure, steam it a little more. Undercooked eggplant is rubbery. Sprinkle eggplant and onion evenly over pizza.

Slide pizza and bottom sheet of parchment onto a rimless cookie sheet, then transfer to the hot baking stone. Bake until pizza edges start to brown and sauce bubbles, about 14 minutes. Use the rimless cookie sheet and a fork to remove pizza safely from the oven.

Cut basil leaves into ribbons and sprinkle over pizza. Pizza is best served hot, but is also good the next day at room temperature for lunch. Refrigerate any extra for up to four days or freeze.

MARKET MANAGER!

Y ou look ready to pop!" Mr. Henry says to Cloe, patting the market manager on her belly. "When is that little codger going to come to see the sunlight?"

"Two weeks, Mr. Henry. I'm due on Labor Day."

"Now that's what I call good timing, gal!"

Two more weeks. In this heat!

The August sun comes up over the movie theater, lighting the tops of the white tents. A mom smoothes sunscreen over her daughter's face before sending her out to play on the Astroturf. I think longingly of my days under an office's florescent lights. It may have been boring, but it was cool and dry!

Peg waves me over. "Sophia, we've got a proposition for you."

"Prop away!"

"You know Cloe is leaving at the end of the month. From the looks of that belly, she may be leaving sooner than that. You've been doing such a good job for me and Mr. Henry and all. We on the market board want to ask you if you'd fill in for Cloe. Here's the offer."

I take the 3 x 5 card from her and look at the figures scrawled in pencil. Three months for twenty hours a week, then three more at fifteen during the cold season.

"We're closed Christmas week, but you'd be paid for that too. And if you can get enough interest to support a bigger winter market, your hours would go up."

I see that the totals would let me keep my place at Park & Market, especially now that I was doing the outreach for five farms. Mr. Henry, bless his heart, had spread the word. And the last time I stopped by for a falafel, the guy who ran the Pita Parade food truck asked me to do his website, too.

It could be one of those elusive win-win-win situations: good for my customers, good for the market, and good for me. And I wouldn't have to take one of those rat-race jobs, air-conditioning or no air-conditioning.

"When do I start?"

Back home, I make a week's worth of gazpacho. I'll top it with peaches plus basil for breakfast and with chickpeas and olives for dinner. Peg told me that cukes usually aren't bitter when it's hot, but I take a bite of a thin slice from each end to test them anyway. Fortunately, they're sweet so I don't have to peel them.

Heat-Wave Gazpacho

Active time: 20 minutes. Total time: 2 hours. Makes about 10 servings, 1 cup each.

2 garlic cloves
1 cup water
¼ cup olive oil
2½ pounds tomatoes, about 4 large, cored but not seeded
2 cucumbers, peeled only if bitter, cut into 3-inch chunks
2 bell peppers, cored, quartered, and seeded
1 yellow onion, peeled and quartered
3 to 4 slices whole-grain bread, torn into chunks
2 tablespoons red wine vinegar
1 teaspoon salt
1 teaspoon cumin
ground black pepper to taste, optional
1 jalapeño pepper, cored, seeded (add half at a time, then taste),
optional
for garnish (optional): peeled and chopped peaches, basil ribbons,
chickpeas, chopped vegetables, olives ...

Drop garlic into a running blender or food processor fitted with
the cutting blade. Let garlic bounce until well chopped then turn
machine off.

Prepare vegetables and process in the machine on high until
smooth, adding all ingredients except for garnish in the order listed.
If the machine won't handle 10 cups easily, work in batches, divid-
ing water, tomatoes, and bread so each batch has enough liquid to
be processed easily.

Pour gazpacho into a large bowl, stir, and taste. Adjust seasonings. Chill thoroughly if you have the patience. Serve in bowls,
topped with your choice of garnish.

PROPER ATTIRE

I tug the apron ties tight, then give myself a sultry glance over my left shoulder and into the full-length mirror.

Lookin' good! crows my inner James Brown as I smooth down the ties on my bare white behind. No need to worry that losing weight would diminish *la derriere*. Switching from Pringles to peppers had helped me drop ten pounds. Then work on the farm toned me up and the lift from my red high heels put the rump I had left at a perky angle.

Roger might not approve of heels at the farmers' market, but let's see what he thinks of them for a very short walk across a carpet!

The bell chimes and I teeter to the door. A quick look out the peephole shows Roger, frowning at a text message on his phone.

He looks up when I open the door.

"Your hair looks like a halo," he said. "But given this outfit, I'm not sure if you are an angel or a devil." He steps into my apartment and pulls the door shut behind him. His strong, tanned hand slides across my bare waist while the other strokes up my spine and then down past the apron ties to my ass.

I feel my nipples strain toward him through the apron's thin cotton.

"Angel in the kitchen and devil in bed," I whisper into his ear. The heels give me just enough extra height that I can catch his earlobe between my teeth.

"We'll see about that," Roger says, lifting me up into his arms and striding toward my bedroom. "Didn't I warn you about walking in such ridiculous shoes?"

"Who's walking?"

The next morning, I ease out of bed without waking Roger and retrieve my crumpled apron. To think it was supposed to protect me from hot and messy things!

I shuffle off to the kitchen wearing the apron and bunny slippers. Good thing I'd baked oatmeal yesterday just in case he stayed for breakfast.

Love-Me-Slender Baked Oatmeal Cake with Fruit
Active time: 20 minutes. Total time: 65 minutes. Serves 8.

¼ cup dried coconut (20 grams)
2 cups old-fashioned rolled oats (160 grams)
1½ teaspoon baking powder
½ teaspoon cinnamon
½ teaspoon salt
¼ teaspoon nutmeg
2 tablespoons finely ground flaxseed (14 grams)
1¼ cup water
1 sweet red cooking apple, such as a Gala
¼ cup honey or sorghum
¼ cup raisins (40 grams)
shortening or canola oil for the pan

Heat oven to 350°F. Oil heart-shaped cake pan and line with parchment cut to fit. (You can also bake this in an 8x8 baking pan or 9-inch cake pan.)

Put coconut in a food processor fitted with a cutting blade and process for about 30 seconds. Add ½ cup oats and pulse five or six times. Put mixture in a medium bowl with remaining oats, baking powder, cinnamon, salt, and nutmeg. Stir to combine.

Put flaxseed and ¼ cup water in a microwave-safe container. Heat until very warm, about one minute on high. Stir to develop eggy texture.

Dice apple while flaxseed mixture cools. Add flaxseed and remaining water to oat mixture, stirring just enough to combine. Stir in apple, sorghum, and raisins. If you're in the mood, use your fingers to arrange apples so most of the red peels show. Bake for 30 to 35 minutes, until oatmeal cake begins to pull away from the edges of the pan and is firm to the touch.

Let oatmeal cake cool in the pan for at least ten minutes, then run a plastic knife between it and the pan to loosen it. Put a plate on top, then flip the baking pan and plate together so the cake falls out of the pan onto the plate. Peel off parchment and flip cake onto a pretty serving plate.

Serve warm or at room temperature. Keeps covered at room temperature for about four days.

FIFTY PERCENT PLUS ONE

It's the weekend after Labor Day. I feel a little nostalgic for my old, air-conditioned job as the first political ads of the season hit the airwaves.

Roger turns off the radio. "Seems like an ugly ad to be running on a bluegrass station." He turns the ceiling fan up a notch. I look at the parched tan grass between us and the barn.

"Back when we were having that little tussle about June and Sally, you said something about 'fifty percent plus plus.' What did you mean?"

"Fifty percent plus one. That's the be-all-and-end-all of modern political campaigns. If you get half the votes plus one, you win the election. Working any harder than that is seen as a fool's game."

"What about the issues?"

"Some candidates really want to serve, and make the world a better place. I admire that even when their definition of better makes me crazy. But others just like the power, or the applause, or the chance for side deals. They know exactly how much each vote costs. That breed works for their donors, not their constituents."

"Was the guy you worked for like that?"

"No, he's one of the good guys. He's doing as best he can in office, but he doesn't need help any more getting elected. And that's why I'm with you today."

"There's a silver lining to everything."

Silver, *feh!* I want chocolate. I rub the twin aches between my belly button and my hip bones. Time to try Charlotte's weird avocado sorbet. She claims it is better than any store-bought chocolate ice cream and *nearly* as good as *Gourmet's* Chocolate Velvet Ice Cream, at a fraction of the time, cost, calories, and clean-up. Just what a gal needs at times like this.

Thirty minutes later I text Charlotte: c why u needed new word, sorbet not enough. pms nixed! xxoo

Chocolate Coldacado

Active time: 10 minutes, plus an optional 30 minutes of occasional handle-turning if you have a manual ice-cream maker to make sorbet. Total time: 10 to 40 minutes. Serves 4.

2 ripe avocadoes
½ cup cocoa, such as Ghirardelli's natural unsweetened cocoa
½ cup sugar
¼ cup full-fat or low-fat coconut milk
1 teaspoon vanilla
⅛ teaspoon chipotle

Quarter and peel avocadoes and remove pits. Put avocado flesh into a food processor fitted with the cutting blade or in a blender.

Add remaining ingredients and process until smooth.

For pudding, serve as is. For sorbet, chill for up to a day if you have time, then process in an ice-cream maker according to the manufacturer's directions. (Pre-chilling makes it freeze faster and should make it smoother, with smaller ice crystals. If you can't wait, don't. The results will still be superb.)

Charlotte freezes the extra in single-serving containers, then packs one with her lunch to help keep it cool. Sometimes she sets one out on the counter to thaw while she eats dinner, so it is still frozen but spoonable.

WAKING UP CRANKY

Hildi and Gullin squeal me awake. I struggle out of tangled sheets and pad into the farmhouse kitchen for caffeine.
Roger pours me a cup of coffee then glops something into bowl.

I push the strange hot cereal away, untouched.

He frowns.

I bite my lip.

He scowls, looking at my lip with an undecipherable expression. Could it be lust? *Ciao amore!* He looked so ... hot!

I smirk and push away the jar of sorghum too.

His eyes darken.

I feel my Lower Forty clench.

I bite my lip again, this time knowing exactly what I am doing. I tuck my chin down and pout in my best virginal-Tess way. Would he finally give me what I'd been asking for?

Um, no. Instead, Roger laughs. "Is that the face that got your Papà to give you the car keys? I thought my Sorghum was a grown-up."

Roger wraps me up in his strong arms and hugs me tight, then rubs my spine briskly with one hand the way he would pet Dolly, Patsy, or June. He murmurs baby talk just above my ear, "Do you want to sulk and spit? Are you a naughty, selfish girl?"

He pulls my hair back and bites my lower lip, first gently and then with growing pressure until I groan. I feel like the cagey and sultry Sophia Loren in *Marriage—Italian Style*. My bathrobe parts as I pulled him closer. Like my namesake, I'm not wearing underwear.

"Then find somebody else to play with," Roger said, releasing me. "Honey, this ain't *Cold Comfort Farm*. If you want to be or make victims in that sort of gossipy life, go back to your political pals in Raleigh."

I wince, thinking of the hours of bickering that had made up so much of my life Before. First with Mamma, then with a string of boyfriends, and finally for years with Kenny. Want to be happy? Then fight first so you can make up.

"No, please. I'll try your weird porridge."

"*Weird porridge?* I set up the slow cooker so you could feast like the ancient Aztecs and Incas, to grow strong like Samurais preparing for battle. This is not some Dickensian gruel, but the super grains the Conquistadors couldn't extinguish."

He catches his breath, then continues, "Take time to smell the cinnamon, Sophia. Eat with gratitude for the farmers and seed savers and all who made your breakfast possible. If you do, I've got a way to work the calories back off that I'm sure you'll enjoy."

I take a big spoonful of the porridge. It's nutty and rich. Raisins make it sweet and amarath has a slight crunch. I chew a bit of kombu and taste the sea.

"Yes, sir. I promise to be grateful for all your gifts."

Ancient Heroes Breakfast Bowl

Active time: 5 minutes. Total time: 8 hours. Serves 4.

1 cup quinoa (170 grams)
1 cup amaranth (190 grams)
5 cups water
½ cup raisins (40 grams)
1 teaspoon cinnamon
¼ teaspoon salt
one 3-inch strip kombu (optional)

Rinse quinoa well to avoid a bitter breakfast and put into slow cooker with remaining ingredients, breaking kombu into half-inch pieces first if using.

Cover slow cooker and turn on low. Cook until grains are tender, about 8 hours.

COLLEGE REUNION

There's a certain sort of late September day that makes me long for a fresh start. This time of year, students revel in new subjects before starting the grind of term papers and tests. Candidates work their circuits hard with finely honed speeches and without the exhausted cynicism that sets in by Halloween.

I want a little fresh myself, so I spend a lazy Sunday morning catching up with my favorite writers: Mark Bittman and Barbara Kingsolver. David Sedaris, who grew up just a few blocks from here. I'm drawn to the book Roger recommended, Wendell Berry's *The Art of the Commonplace*.

I suddenly I have too much in my head to be alone. I text Roger: **Dinner @ 7? I'll cook.**

Roger texts back: **UR on!**

I can make pasta and salad at Roger's place. I want him to try the new salad dressing I've been using on everything from cooked collards to baked potatoes this week.

That night, we talk and talk, from the time Roger opens the door of my Prius to nearly midnight. He's surprisingly informed on politics, especially on green issues. We talk about the seismic changes in our world: global warming, overpopulation, Frankenfoods.

It feels like the college days again, with all the world before us. Only now, the future was dark. I'd helped good politicians get into office, but they hadn't been able to make the kind of changes we'd hoped for, at least not fast enough.

I'm glad we have so many ways to help give them more time. Even trivial actions like saving salad scraps for compost can preserve the world. *Un pochino*; a tiny bit.

Smoky Tomato-Tahini Salad Dressing

Active time: 5 minutes. Total time: 5 minutes. Makes 1 cup.

1 clove garlic
1 cup fire-roasted crushed tomatoes (244 grams)
2 tablespoons tahini (30 grams)
1 teaspoon apple cider vinegar
¼ teaspoon ground chipotle

Set up your food processor with the cutting blade or use a blender. Peel garlic, turn food processor on high, and drop garlic into food processor, letting the machine run until the garlic stops bouncing around.

Add remaining ingredients and process until smooth. Taste and adjust seasonings.

Serve within four hours or refrigerate for up to four days.

WEASELS OR ANGELS?

Nicole pops three blueberries from my sample dish just as I start to close down the booth for the day. Isn't she supposed to be feeding the poor?

"Can I help you?"

"No, I'm good. Just looking for Rog."

No good, I think, emptying the bowls before she can take more. "He's getting the truck. Can I help you?"

"Would you let him know that my boyfriend can give me a ride home after all?"

"I didn't know you had a boyfriend."

"Same one since tenth grade. He's been away this summer interning for a company that makes produce boxes from recycled plastic bags. Rog is his angel."

Now I am really confused. I thought Nicole had the hots for Farmer Bee, but now she telling me that he's got a thing going with her boyfriend? She doesn't seem upset, though, so maybe I shouldn't be either.

"If he's your boyfriend, shouldn't *you* be his angel?"

"I'm his love-bunny, but I don't have anything like the money takes to be somebody's angel investor. That takes a cool half mil, easy."

Stranger and stranger! "Roger Branch has five hundred *thousand* dollars, in US currency, for someone else?"

"That and more. He's funded five or six companies that are part of the Piedmont foodshed: Real Deal Seeds, the Conscious Cafe, the co-op, Freda's Fine Pickles. Rog says something about how keeping his money local makes it echo. Echo? Maybe breed. All I know is that he's helping my Boo's dream come true."

Nicole does a little out-of-orbit spin, giggles, and pats my arm just the way I've seen her pat Roger. Suddenly I see her as a giggly girl in love, not as a threat.

She waltzes away, stopping by Mr. Henry's booth to flirt with the old man. Why hadn't I recognized her behavior after all my years around candidates seeking donation?

Blueberry Slump

Active time: 20 minutes. Total time: 50 minutes. Serves 8.

1 quart blueberries (600 grams)
½ cup sugar (100 grams)
⅓ cup water
1 cup Good Baking Mix (120 grams) (page 44)
⅛ teaspoon cinnamon
⅛ teaspoon nutmeg
⅛ teaspoon cardamom
1 tablespoon sugar
⅓ cup water
½ cup Cashew Cream (optional) (page 90)

Pick through blueberries, removing stems and any moldy or very hard ones. Rinse and put in a wide skillet with water, sugar, and spices. Cover and bring to a boil. Reduce heat to low so berries just simmer while you make dumplings.

Stir baking mix, sugar, and spices in a medium bowl until well combined. Stir in water with as few strokes as possible, until only a few lumps remain.

Gently place eight or so even dollops of dough on top of simmering blueberry sauce, avoiding splashing blueberry juice on the dumplings. (Match the number of dollops to the number of servings desired.) Do not stir. Cover pot and allow dumplings to steam undisturbed until cooked through, about 30 minutes.

To serve, ladle a dumpling and the fruit it rests on into a dessert bowl. Top with a spoonful of Cashew Cream if desired. Best eaten immediately, but keeps refrigerated for a day or two. Microwave briefly to reheat.

SLOW MONEY, HONEY

I hear you've been giving away bags of money."

"Not guilty," Roger tells me. Roger pulls on the Frisbee until Dolly releases it, then throws it back into the yard. All three border collies race after it. The sun is starting to set. The chickens are heading into the shelter of their gypsy trailer before it gets dark.

"Don't make me put Nicole on the stand. She said you gave somebody named Boo a half-million dollars."

Roger laughs. "If you ask Albert, I think you'll find that he only tolerates Nicole calling him 'Boo.' I'm not giving him money, I'm investing in his new company. He's got a great idea for making re-usable boxes out of recycled plastic bottles. They're light-weight and can be sanitized, too, so the farmers save money and the food is safer. Albert is going to more than repay me in a few years. He's going to put some of those textile workers back in the game, too."

"What about the others?"

"More of the same. I don't expect to make back as much off some of them, but there are other benefits. Harry is breeding some beyond-tasty peppers. Freda may take longer, but having her pickling operation in place will let me sell cukes as bread-and-butter pickles. Hildi and Gullin will just have to eat something else."

"Nicole says that your money echoes."

"The echo may be in that sweet girl's head. The money amplifies — becomes more powerful — because we all help each other."

"But so much money! And so many businesses!"

"A guy's got to have a hobby. Think of me as being like the game master for a role-playing game. My secret power is finding ways that let everybody win. Turns out the best way to make your investors happy is to make all the other stakeholders happy, from your customers and employees to your suppliers and the community."

"Do you have big bags of gold in your basement?"

Roger shot me a glance, then shook his head. "No, no bags of gold anywhere. I just use it as seed corn to plant another field.

But tonight I think I'll blow some of it trying to impress a beautiful woman. How about dinner at the Conscious Cafe? The new chef just graduated from the community college's Natural Chef program."

"Will you be expecting a big return on that investment?" I ask, batting my eyes.

"All indicators predict a bull market."

Roger snorts, paws the floor with one foot, and wiggles his index fingers over his head like the horns of a very horny bull. He charges and I run for the least-safe place in the house, his king-sized bed.

Fortunately, the Conscious Cafe stays open late.

Sweet-and-Tart Collard Tangle

Active time: 20 minutes. Total time: at least 20 minutes, ideally 2 hours and 20 minutes. Serves 8.

12 ounces collards (340 grams or about 8 medium leaves)
2 tablespoons lemon juice (juice from one lemon)
1 teaspoon olive oil
¼ teaspoon salt
⅛ teaspoon freshly ground pepper
1 sweet apple, perhaps a Gala or Fuji
¼ cup walnut pieces (27 grams)
¼ cup raisins (40 grams)

Cut or pull stems away from collard leaves and save stems for another use. Cut leaves into very thin strips by stacking and rolling leaves up like a cigar, then cutting crossways. Put leaves into a glass or ceramic salad bowl or similar non-reactive container.

With clean and loving hands, gently squeeze and massage collards five or six times until they relax a bit. Inhale their deep green fragrance and admire your wild collard tangle.

In a small bowl, mix lemon juice, olive oil, salt, and pepper. Pour dressing over collard tangle and toss until well coated and glossy. For best results, cover and refrigerate for at least two hours before finishing the recipe.

Core apple, slice, and cut into small pieces. Chop walnuts if needed. Toss fruit and nuts with collard leaves, making sure to coat the apple pieces well so they don't brown.

Serve at once or refrigerate. Keeps without browning or losing its chewy spring for several days.

NATURE, NURTURE, OR NASTY?

C ome *on*, Jo Lynn," I beg. "If you keep fussing with your hat, we'll be late for the parade!"

"I'm not going to be runner-up for Pepper Queen again this year. I'm going to show Mr. Simms what North Carolina royalty looks like."

She glowers at me, but it's hard to take a scolding seriously when it comes from someone wearing an outfit made mostly from peppers.

Pretty funny, I think. But not much funnier than the British Queen Mum's boxy purses and adoring corgis. Jo Lynn is certainly ready to compete. Hat festooned with a rainbow of peppers, baby squash, and rosemary? Check. Flowing dress made from pepper-print cotton? Check. Jewelry made from dried peppers and seeds? Check. She'd even inked peppers on her white Toms shoes.

It felt odd to have Mr. Simms drive us in his van instead of the Butler Shuttler, but in less than an hour we are being waved through the gates of Briar Chapel. This wasn't the sort of gated community that I'd been to before for fundraisers, bristling with McMansions. Here, the stone and wood homes blended in with their surroundings and hybrids outnumbered Hummers.

"Busman's holiday," says Mr. Simms as he gets on the shuttle that takes us from the parking lot to the village green. We hear the root-groove band before we see it. Jo Lynn and Mr. Simms line up for the parade. I spot Roger watching the hula-hoopers and fire-dancers perform. I sneak up behind him and give him a hug.

"Just in time, Sorghum," he says, turning to kiss me. "They're starting dance lessons in a minute."

We dance until we're breathless, then head to the tasting line to try dozens of pepper varieties and dishes. Even pepper beer!

Jo Lynn's outfit and enthusiasm win over the judges. Pepper Queen at last. Mr. Simms bows deeply as he ushers her into his van.

Roger whispers in my ear, "Behold Her Hot Majesty, Queen of the Capsaicin. I bet Simms finds her at the top of the Scofield scale tonight."

"I want to be on top too."

Freezing Peppers

To get peppers ready for the freezer, rinse well, cut out the stem, seeds, and white parts inside, and chop into half-inch pieces. To remove the extra seeds clinging to the inside of the pepper, just dipped the pepper halves into a bowl of water. The seeds rinse away and float to the bottom, so the same bowl of water will be good for a bag full of peppers. No more tedious picking at the seeds or clogged drain! Compost the seedy water along with the pepper scraps.

To finish freezing, spread pepper pieces in a single layer on a cookie sheet. Freeze for several hours until solid. Use a spatula to loosen peppers from sheet, then put in a labeled freezer-weight plastic bag, suck out the extra air with a straw, and seal. Pop bags of peppers in your freezer and make sure to note your harvest on your freezer inventory.

FRESH AIR

These sandals practically walk off the shelf all by themselves," Connie tells me as she slides on the other Jambu sandal. I'm taking a break from the booth to catch the fall sale at Comfortable Soles, just down the street from the Starbucks. "This turquoise shows off your peachy pedicure, too."

As I slip my new sandals on and put my old ones in the bag, I ask, "May I use your rest room for a second?"

"We don't have a public one ..."

I look at Connie with a twinkle that somehow convinces her to relent. "OK, use the staff restroom. But be discreet or we'll have a line."

"*Discreet* is my middle name."

I slip past the stacks of shoe boxes to the staff restroom. I slide my panties down my legs and off. I put the small silky bundle in my purse, touch up my lipstick, and fluff up my hair. My new shorter cut gives me a nimbus of waves, feminine but out of the way.

"Ciao, Connie," I say as I sashay out the door and back to Roger. My flowered skirt swings teasingly across my bare body. A puff of breeze lifts it up, almost dangerously, but I just enjoy the unusually naked feeling and let my skirt go where it blows.

This is what love feels like, I think as I work my way through the crowd. People seem to notice. Pheromones or attitude? Who cares! I'm sexy and I know it.

Roger looks up from wrapping three bunches of basil for the chef from Spring Rolls. He keeps on looking. I smile even more broadly and come around to his side of the display.

"Damn, Sorghum!" he said huskily. "You look like Penelope Cruz today. Maybe like the goddess Flora herself."

I reach into my purse, palm my still-warm panties, and slip them into his hand. Discreetly, just as I told Connie.

He looks at me with astonishment and desire, then runs his hand down my hip from waist to thigh to check. I wink and stand on tiptoe to whisper in his ear.

"*Commanda!*"

Light Summer Pesto

Active time: 10 minutes. Total time: 10 minutes. Serves 8.

4 garlic cloves
2 cups tightly packed basil leaves (50 grams)
2 tablespoons nutritional yeast (nooch)
½ teaspoon salt
1½ cups walnut halves and pieces (165 grams)
¾ cups olive oil

Drop garlic into a running blender or food processor fitted with the cutting blade. Let garlic bounce until well chopped then turn machine off.

Add basil leaves, nutritional yeast, and salt, then add walnuts to help hold leaves down. Process until well chopped, scraping down the sides if needed. Pour in olive oil in a thin stream while the machine runs. Process until pesto is as smooth as you like.

Toss with hot pasta, spread on bread or toast, or mix into cooked vegetables and soups just before serving.

Pesto darkens when exposed to air, so press plastic wrap onto it or cover with a thin layer of oil before refrigerating or freezing.

Freeze in muffin tins or ice-cube trays. Dip the bottoms of the frozen containers in warm water for a few seconds, then pop out frozen pesto blocks. Quickly put them in freezer-weight bags, suck out the air, and freeze for up to six months.

BEE-WILDERED

Farmer Bee? Roger?" I call louder this time. He said he'd be home, but the farmhouse seems deserted. I feel a creeping dread. Farming can be dangerous. What if he'd fallen into a thresher or whatever those big machines in the barn were?

I set the jar of borscht on the counter and check the bathroom and bedroom, heart pounding. What if he'd passed out before he could get help? Returning to the kitchen, I see June laying down in the hall, front paws and nose pointed toward the broom closet. A light shines out beneath its door.

"Roger? Farmer Bee?" A second door opens on narrow wood stairs going down to a rough cement-walled basement. I creep down the stairs and look around the corner, afraid of what I might find. What I see next makes me feel like Alice down the rabbit hole, looking at a world I hadn't dreamed existed.

Roger is there, but suddenly he's no Farmer Bee. He's wearing a finely tailored suit jacket over what looks like a silk knit shirt in deep green, just a shade darker than his eyes. Stranger still, he sits in the Borg-like embrace of a multi-layered desk made of brushed aluminum tubes and sleek birchwood, every surface stacked with keyboards, joysticks, or giant computer monitors. I don't see any sacks of gold from his business investments, but this level of elegance and technology doesn't come cheap.

He's talking — Skyping? — to five other people. The man and woman who appear on one monitor have the same uber-stylish look as Roger. The other three look like volunteers for a late-night phone bank, with ironic t-shirts and scruffy beards.

Roger nods attentively as an Indian man makes a point about market share, but below the desk his hand shoos me to the edge of the room. Stunned, I move over to a trophy case full of action figures and wooden artists' models.

On the other side of the big glass sliding doors behind Roger, I see a walled, formal garden. It must be cut into the hill behind the house like one of those British ha-has that keeps cattle from getting too near the manor houses. A stone Japanese lantern lights the raked gravel and small pool. I wince when a big koi leaps into the moonlight, creating a ring of ripples when it splashes down.

You never know what lay beneath the surface.

Now one of the geeks in ball caps is arguing about release dates. Roger steals a glance at me and make the circular gesture that means "Wrap it up, Buddy!"

The rest of the room is hung with framed movie posters and shelves holding boxes of computer games. Looking closer, I see that all of them are signed:

> *Thanks for pulling our asses out of the fire, Rog!*
> *We never would have won without your snake trick!!!*
> *Best dad-gum character wrangler on the Ranch!*

I am dying to check out the wall of framed photos, but that would put me in full view of the video conference callers.

Finally, Roger signs off and swivels around in his black mesh chair. He puts his hands behind his head, leans back and grins.

"OK, you caught me."

"But caught you at what? Are you the Mr. Hyde to my Farmer Bee?"

"Simply an animator, Madam," he said, standing up and giving me a sweeping bow. "The man who made Princess Tatania slay the Nardak, Gangly George swing with the apes, and caused grown men to cry when Little Laslo perished. How do you think I could afford eighty acres of prime Piedmont farmland?"

Blender Borscht

The deep vivid color, the slight sweetness with an underlying earthiness, and a swirl of Cashew Cream on top makes borscht one romantic soup. Dish up a cool bowlful, put *Dr. Zhivago* on, and forget the heat.

Active time: 20 minutes. Total time: 30 minutes. Serves 8.

1 pound beets
1 cup water
2 cups very roughly chopped green cabbage
2 cups Bonus Broth (page 121) or other vegetable broth
2 tablespoons lemon juice
½ teaspoon salt
Cashew Cream for garnish (page 90)

Scrub beets and poke all over with a fork so steam can escape as they cook. Put them in a microwave-safe container with water and microwave on high for about 15 minutes. Let rest, covered, for 10 minutes. Beets should be fork-tender.

Meanwhile, microwave cabbage in a covered, microwave-safe container on high for 7 minutes or until soft.

Uncover beets, cut in half, and let cool. Put the now-purple water in a blender along with the cabbage, broth, lemon juice, and salt. Peel beets and add to blender, saving one if you want to slice thin for garnish. Cover blender and process soup until smooth.

Chill for at least an hour. Serve garnished with beet slices and Cashew Cream, if using.

FLIGHT PATH

I still don't get it, Roger!" I said a week later when my rounds at the market bring me to his booth. The market wouldn't open for twenty more minutes. I'd brought us each a big cup of coffee to help fight the chill.

"I googled your projects. You must have had fun, big time fun, in California. I mean, working on Skywalker Ranch! Then winning all those awards after you broke off to start your own company."

I tug my rain hood further down my forehead. It's the first cold day of fall and the rain makes it feel colder. Only our most dedicated customers venture out in this kind of weather. Those who do will find good bargains on apples, peppers, and winter squash plus the first of the cool-season greens.

"I got into the business because I loved the idea of expressing the physics in the beauty and movement of nature. Princess Tatania shows you what my poor imagination conjured up when trying to think of the most beautiful of all possible women — before you showed me how much better the real world could be. I loved making the graphics that showed how her hair rippled in the wind, and how she leapt from a racing wagon onto the back of a running horse."

He pauses and looks into the distance, over the top of the stores and into the thunderclouds.

"We sold our little graphics startup to a big media company, which we all thought would give us the resources do to even more interesting projects. But they wanted blockbusters for teenaged boys just getting hooked on the rush of violence and sex. Sometimes violent sex, too."

Roger pastes on a welcoming smile to give a CSA box to a long-time customer, then steps back where the tent provides better shelter from the rain.

"When I found out they were using my physics to create rape scenes, I felt sick. I went to my sister's for Thanksgiving. Thought maybe coming back to my roots would me get past the anger and decide what to do."

He cleared his throat and looked at the kids playing on the Astroturf.

"It did. I'd brought a new baseball mitt for my nephew Joey, but he wouldn't come outside to play catch. Wouldn't even walk down to the river to look for turtles. Sis had to threaten to whale him good to get him to put stop playing computer games and eat Thanksgiving dinner. He sure did eat, though. Gained ten pounds of fat since I'd seen him last year."

"Then my ex-wife wrote a book on the 'shocking truth' about how hard pixel factories are on families. Some fan girl figured out that I was the guy my ex called Hud in her book. This girl then posted pictures of me just out minding my own business. Out walking my dog or at a basketball game with friends. I felt hunted. She even went to technical conferences when I was speaking to ask fake questions, ones that were really about my love-life with Ellen. Like 'was the ice-cube trick really as effective as claimed?'"

He winks at me and I blush. It was remarkably effective.

"So I decided to cash out my stock and get into farming. I started as an apprentice with the Johnsons and the Carters, then bought this place when my cousin Elon got too old to farm."

He tucks a curly black lock back under my hood and leans down to give me a quick kiss.

"Are you still helping them make these not-quite-X games?" I ask.

"I've got one more year of consulting on my contract and then I'm free. I still like messing around with physics and graphics on my own, especially in the winter when the farm doesn't need as much attention. But lately I've been more interested in seeing how a particular real woman looks when she's being brave or happy."

"Or wet," I say, opening up my umbrella to go to the welcome booth. It was time for the market to open.

"Or wet. When this is over, let's go home to see if I can make you so happy you *like* being wet."

"Make that cold and wet, if you've got any ice cubes."

Core Recipe: Homemade Apple Cider Vinegar
Active time: 5 minutes. Total time: 6 weeks. Makes about 1 cup.

1 cup apple cores and, optionally, peels
2 tablespoons sugar
1 cup water

Find a glass or ceramic container and a glass or ceramic plate or other container that fits just inside the first one. Run the containers through the dishwasher or dip them into boiling water to get them very clean.

Put apple cores, peels if using, and sugar in the larger container. Add water so apple parts are covered by about an inch. Stir. Put second container on top to keep the apple parts from poking up into the air. Cover with a clean tea towel and let ferment in a dark place at room temperature (60° to 85°F) for a week.

Every few days, stir the mixture and spoon off any mold. Enjoy the bubbles that will start to form and don't worry about the mold: it's normal.

Pour mixture through a clean strainer into very clean jar. Cover with clean cloth, such as cheese cloth, a bit of cotton, or a scrap of old pantyhose. Secure fabric with a rubber band or the ring from a canning jar. Store in a cool, dark place for about six weeks.

Replace the fabric with a solid lid and store vinegar in a dark place. Keeps indefinitely.

Don't worry about the ghostly mother of vinegar that may be floating in the jar. It's not only harmless, many people believe it has healing properties. If the mother bothers you, pour your vinegar through a coffee filter or cheesecloth into another very clean container.

Use vinegar as desired for salad dressings, cooking, homemade vegetable spray, and cleaning.

Don't use it for preserving other food unless you have a way to test its strength. It might not be fierce enough to keep your food safe over long periods.

COMMUNITY, NOT CUSTOMERS

I button up the jacket Mamma gave me last Christmas, amazed that it is a little loose now, even though I've got a warm wool sweater underneath. I check out my layered look in the mirror: perfect for a brisk November morning.

The farm stands will be loaded with produce picked in anticipation of the first hard frost of the year. The Abundance Foundation let me use the winning pepper recipes in a handout for the market customers today. Maybe some of them will fill their freezers with ripe local peppers like I had. Even organic peppers were a great investment just before the frost hit. Buy low, eat high!

Sally Johnson and Ruth Carter are among the first to pick up a flyer. I hold my arms out for Baby Chip, who burbles and smiles. Ruth's daughter Riley shows me her doll's new dress.

"We're shopping big for a party today," says Sally. "My sister Brittany is back from Afghanistan. She should be driving up from Fort Bragg right now."

"I'm so happy for you!"

"Me too! I'm so glad she made it back safe. And her girls here are just going wild with the thought of seeing Mommy again."

"Mommy! Mommy!" shout Riley and her sister Mia, holding hands and jumping up and down. "Mommy's coming home!" Baby Chip claps and laughs. I wipe a little drool from his chin with his Eat Local bib, then hand him back to Ruth. As they head off to shop, I realized I can name every one of their kids and can say whether they belong to Sally, June, or Brittany. If *belong* is even the right word in such a warm mix of friends and family. Heck, just now it felt like Baby Chip belonged to me, at least just a little.

Jo Gore is singing happy jazz on the square, a tune from her new CD. Bo exudes serious jazz cool behind his sunglasses as he takes over with a solo verse on his acoustic guitar. Kids tumble and dance to the music while their parents sip coffee on the edges of the green.

I scan the rest of the market. There's Mary Beth Hardison with the first winter squash of the season. Buck totes a bag full of greens for juicing over to the health club. I don't see a blur of sticky kids to be avoided or cynical adults to be cajoled into giving up their votes or money. Some are friends, some are, are … isn't there a warmer word than *stakeholders*?

I drop that thought as Roger walks up to the welcome booth to check in for the week.

And one is my lover. The right one, this time.

"Come out to the farm tomorrow?" he asks. "I've got something to show you."

Tender Tangle

If you are cooking for someone who prefers softer food or just if you grow tired of eating chewy raw Sweet-and-Tart Collard Tangle (page 154), steam it briefly to further relax the leaves and bring out the sweetness of the fruit.

Put as much of the Tangle as you'd like in a steamer over the stove and steam for about 5 minutes. You can also microwave it with a teaspoon or two of water in a covered container on high for about 45 seconds per serving.

Cook once, enjoy several times!

BEE AND BEE?

I'm here," I say, huffing a little after climbing the hill.
"Yes, you are," says Roger as he takes my hand in his. "Catch your breath and look with me."

He stands strong and straight in his flannel and denim, with the setting sun catching the silver streaks in his short black hair. I tear my eyes from him and look where he looks, across the gently rolling fields.

A field of rainbow chard lies immediately before us, rows curved with the hills to prevent erosion. Beyond is a field green with Australian peas. It's adding nitrogen and holding down the soil now, but soon I'll be able to snip some for stir fries. Wooded areas follow Varnell Creek and create windbreaks between fields.

Roger gazes beyond the boundaries of the Bee's Knees Farm. "Old man Johnson wants to sell his place. I'm thinking about buying it."

He turns and looks at me deeply, searchingly has he had during our first meeting at the farmers' market. "He's got an old barn that we could fix up as stables. And his farmhouse goes way back. Some of the boards are even made from chestnut, back before the blight. What do you think about fixing it up? The farm house would make a great B&B. We could have horses, invite people out to ride, eat, live the farm life."

"We?"

"Yes, Sophia. We. You love horses and people. I love the land. And I love you, more than anything or anyone." He holds my head in his hands and kissed me thoroughly, wrapping me in his arms as the kiss goes on and on. I tingle from the roots of my hair down through the soles of my feet. Could it be that the charge between us enters the very earth? He pulls me closer as I moan with desire and joy.

Roger comes up for air and holds arms' length. "Can't you see it? If we get started now, we could open it up during the big farm tour in April. The state ag department has all sorts of support for what they call 'agro-tourism.' We can ask Lucy to live there. She's always wanted to make Loco Local a real restaurant, not just a sandwich stand. She can cook up what we grow and her girls can help with the housekeeping."

His enthusiasm is magnetic. I see why folks starting up businesses want to work with him. He makes the crazy seem like a sure thing.

"But the thing that will make it work is you," he says.

Molto dolce! My knees go weak but I don't stumble.

"You can pull it all together. Talk nice to the visitors where I'd tell them to watch where they put their big feet. Make sure Lucy tells you when she needs help. Spread the word like you did for the market. Bring people here, together. Be here with me."

"What exactly are you asking me, Roger?" I was flabbergasted, mind in all directions like dandelion seeds in the wind.

"Marry me, Sophia. Marry me and come to my farm. Our farm! Find horses you will love and bring them here. Check in on Lucy but stay with me, where the tourists won't make me crazy. Let's create a life together, for us and our animals and our land."

He flings his arms wide as the sunset flames behind him. I look over the fields and picture it. Kids learning to ride, families learning to garden. Charlotte can have some cooking classes. We'll have bonfires with the Wilber Brothers playing. A dude *farm* instead of a dude ranch."

I blink back tears of joy. "Yes, Roger, yes!"

He hoots with pleasure and lifts me up, spinning around so I see the setting sun, his house, the woods, the fields, the chickens and pigs and dogs, and our new place. I hold tight, ready for the ride of my life.

Rainbow Love Stew

Rainbow Love Stew is pretty much all you need, at least once a day. This beautifully balanced mix of colorful vegetables and hardy beans builds bones and muscles, keeps your eyes bright, and gives you the energy for a lively life. I like to make a big pot and freeze some for busy times ahead.

Active time: 30 minutes, starting with cooked beans. Total time: 1 hour. Makes 20 servings with three variations.

2 pounds dried pinto beans, cooked (page 23)
1 bunch rainbow chard
4 carrots
2 yellow onions
8 garlic cloves
1 tablespoon olive oil
1 teaspoon ground chipotle

mix-ins
2 oranges
¼ cup raisins (40 grams)
one 28-ounce can diced fire-roasted tomatoes

Cook pintos until nearly tender. Separate chard stems from leaves. Cut any wide stems into ½-inch strips, then cut crossways into ½-inch wide pieces. Cut carrots lengthwise into quarters then cut crosswise into ¼-inch wide pieces. Chop onion. Stir chopped vegetables into beans and continue to simmer. Cut chard leaves into ribbons and set aside.

Mince garlic and put into a microwave-safe container, then stir in olive oil and chipotle. Microwave on high until fragrant, about 40 seconds. Stir garlic mixture and chard leaves into beans and simmer until beans and vegetables are tender, about 30 minutes. Taste and add salt or more chipotle as needed.

Make the first variation by ladling 8 servings (about 8 cups) into storage or freezer containers. Zest oranges on top of these servings, top with raisins, and stir. Let sit at least 20 minutes to allow orange flavor to settle in, then taste and adjust seasons.

Meanwhile, serve or set aside 4 servings of stew to eat as is over baked white potatoes, with oranges on the side. Stir tomatoes into remaining 8 servings. Serve hot in a bowl over baked or microwaved white potatoes.

Serve rest as a soup or over corn bread, white or sweet potatoes, brown rice, or quinoa. Keeps refrigerated for up to a week and frozen for at least a year.

BUT WAIT, THERE'S MORE …

Roger clangs his coffee mug down on the counter and curses. He pushes his phone into his pocket and walks over to the window looking across the Varnell Creek.

I look up from my iPad, where I've been looking at rescue horses for the Bee's Knees B&B. So many horses need homes! Folks who lost their jobs are losing their animals as well as their homes.

"What's wrong, Farmer Bee?"

"Frellin' fracking! Looks like Bob Twaite wants to sell out to those natural gas speculators. If the legislation goes through and he gets his price, we'll have drilling just across the river. Explosions when they break up the bedrock to free the gas."

"Will it be noisy enough to make the horses bolt?"

"Maybe. And there's more. Instead of woods and rolling corn fields across the way, we'll have a mining operation. Trucks shipping miners in and waste water out will clog the roads. Fracking can even pollute the groundwater."

"Yikes! No water, no farm."

"That's right." He turned to me with a determined look. "We've got to stop it."

"Whatever you say, Farmer Bee."

"I'm serious. You've got friends in high places and a thousand people on your mailing list."

"Many more that a thousand," I say. "But let's start in person, with our neighbors. They're the ones with the most at stake." I tell Flicka, "Dial Peg."

A few rings later, I say, "Peg, can you come over for dinner tonight? Roger and I are having some folks over to talk about this new fracking thing. Looks like it might happen right next to us and to Eden Farms."

After a few more calls, I roll up my sleeves and consider what sort of dessert will best encourage people to sign a petition and call their legislators.

I think about what Steve Jobs said about doing what you love in life and not settling. I'm so happy to have found a love and life that uses everything I have and gives me back more pleasure than I thought was possible. I'll do whatever it takes to keep Roger, the farm, and our friends safe.

Don't Settle Apple-Walnut Crumble

Active time: about 30 minutes. Total time: about an hour. Serves 6 to 8.

2 pounds Granny Smith or other tart baking apples, about 5 medium apples (900 grams)
¼ cup white sugar (50 grams)
¼ teaspoon cinnamon
¼ teaspoon nutmeg
pinch salt
¼ cup Earth Balance Coconut Spread or coconut oil (57 grams)
½ cup white whole wheat flour or all-purpose flour (60 grams)
½ cup walnuts (50 grams)
⅓ cup brown sugar (67 grams)
2 tablespoons water

Heat oven to 400°F. Grease an 8-inch square baking pan.

Cut each apple into quarters and cut out the core. Save the cores to make apple cider vinegar (page 179).

Slice each quarter into four long slices, then cut slices across three or four times. Put apple pieces into baking pan as you go.

Mix sugar, cinnamon, nutmeg, and salt in a small bowl. Sprinkle over apples.

Mix flour and brown sugar in the bowl used for sugar mixture. Chop walnuts and stir into flour mixture. Melt coconut spread in a microwave-safe container, about 30 seconds on high. Pour spread over flour mixture and stir until all flour is coated, then crumble over top of apples.

Pour water into container used to melt coconut spread, swish around to pick up remaining flavor, and pour into pan along the edge without wetting the topping.

Bake for 35 to 40 minutes, until topping browns slightly and apples are fork tender. Let cool for at least 10 minutes.

Serve warm and dream big. Keeps covered at room temperature for a few days. Reheat briefly for a perfect breakfast on a day filled with important and satisfying work, friendships, and love.

ACKNOWLEDGEMENTS

With amazed thanks to the team behind this book:

- My husband Bruce Watson, who helped in myriad ways.
- Farmers Haruka and Jason Oatis of Edible Earthscapes, for the delectable introduction to CSAs, with special thanks to Haruka for her comments on the final draft.
- Editor Megan Hustad of Wherewithal Press, who took out fluff and added zing.
- My Wildly Good recipe testers, for making the recipes better: Susan Ball, Jean Connor, Catherine Doran, Suzi Guilford, Julie Harris, Donna Kraft, Jen Michaels, Matthew Miller, Janet Schneider, and Pat Stowe.
- Farmer Wilma Schroeder, bee advocate June Stoyer, sustainable-farming advocate Alice Alexander, and attorney Rob Gelbum, who kept my facts straight.
- Language advisers Melissa Peil, Rossana Palummieri Maldonado, and Mr. Palummieri, who made sure Sophia's Italian is *perfetto*.
- Eagle-eyed Philippa Charlton, for scrutinizing the final draft.
- Martha Grove Hipskind, the Midtown Raleigh Alliance, and the people of Midtown for inspiration.

Any errors that remain are my own.

With gratitude to Denny and Rebecca Reid for adjusting my course. With joy to Quail Ridge Books & Music, the Not Just Desserts Book Club, the Carolina Farm Stewardship Association, Cook for Good supporters, and all my friends for helping me live the life of Cindy Lou.

Index